WEDDING CAKE WIPEOUT - CHRISTIAN COZY MYSTERY

A MOLLY GREY MYSTERY

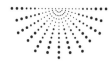

DONNA DOYLE
PURE READ

© 2018 PUREREAD LTD

PUREREAD.COM

CONTENTS

INTRODUCTION

A PERSONAL WORD FROM PUREREAD

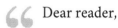 Dear reader,

Do you love a good mystery? So do we! Nothing is more pleasing than a page turner that keeps you guessing until the very last page.

In our Christian cozy mysteries you can be certain that there won't be any gruesome or gory scenes, swearing or anything else upsetting, just good clean fun as you unravel the mystery together with our marvelous characters.

Thank you for choosing PureRead!

～

Love Free Books?
Join our free Cozy Mystery Club Today!
TO RECEIVE MYSTERY CLUB UPDATES, FREE
BOOKS AND SPECIAL OFFERS GO TO
PureRead.com/cozy-mystery-club

A DISASTROUS WEDDING

Calmhaven, June 12
The day of the wedding.

At first people thought it was a prank.

An ill-chosen joke, concocted no doubt by the groom, Billy Monroe. That man was known for his morbid sense of humor, and he somehow must have talked his father-in-law, Abe Mortimer, into behaving like a clown on the day of the wedding.

And truth be told, at first when everyone still thought it was a joke, it was indeed a little funny, seeing the man making weird faces while sputtering, turning bright red and keeling over.

But surely it was all a dumb stunt as nobody ever chokes on a piece of soft, spongy wedding-cake.

But Abe Mortimer did.

After Billy had served his father-in-law a sumptuous piece of the cake, and the jolly, old man had taken a huge bite with shiny eyes, the trouble began. First he turned red, and he coughed, puffed and rattled. It caused some of the guests to let out an obedient chuckle. After all, when the father of the bride cracks a joke, one is supposed to laugh, and with an irresponsible young man like Billy Monroe as your son-in-law, jokes like this can be expected.

Of course the champagne did not help either. Apparently, Abe Mortimer had given himself permission to start on the sparkling wine early, even though the party was only half over, the man had already downed several glasses of the bubbly stuff. On a day like this though, much could be forgiven.

But then, when he began to wildly sway his arms around, his mouth covered with the sweet, sticky cream from the cake, and he hit the top layer of the cake with his right fist, thus effectively destroying the culinary marvel of master cake maker Albert Finney, people began to wonder.

This was not a joke at all.

Something was terribly wrong and poor Abe Mortimer was in trouble. A piece of cake had gotten stuck in the wrong pipe, and he needed help!

People began to scream left and right.

"A doctor," Billy Monroe screamed, not knowing what else to do. "Is there a doctor around?"

One of the waiters showed great presence of mind, and ran up with a glass of red wine so Abe Mortimer could clear the sugary rubble in his lungs. But it was too little, too late.

As Abe jerked the glass out of the waiter's hand and gulped down the exquisite Musigny Gran Cru 2012, he gurgled and sank to his knees. The wineglass slipped out of his hand and shattered in a thousand pieces on the floor.

The bride, Charmayne Mortimer, let out a scream and ran to her Daddy. Not caring about her wedding dress, she dropped to her knees and took her Daddy's head in her arms. "Please, Daddy... " She turned around and cried in a hysterical, high-pitched voice, "Somebody help...! Please... Daddy is not well."

And then, right when Abe Mortimer looked into the face of his beloved daughter, he relaxed, and something that could be classified as a very weak smile appeared on his face. It happened right before paramedics, running through the bewildered guests, scooped the old man up onto a stretcher and rushed him outside to the waiting ambulance. A terrified hush settled over the wedding room. Was the irrepressible Abe Mortimer.... dead?

For what seemed like an eternity, but was no doubt no more than a few seconds, nobody even spoke, and besides the tune of "Love is in the Air," that was playing through the speakers in the background, not a sound was heard. No one could believe that dear Abe Mortimer, the well-known Mayor of the town of Calmhaven, had left the building in such a shocking way.

What an unfortunate accident. And during the wedding of Charmayne and Billy Monroe. Things couldn't be worse.

Nobody at the wedding of Abe's only daughter knew what to say. All they could do now was pray. There were no words to describe what had happened.

And Molly Gertrude Grey did pray. "Lord, save your servant, Abe. Spare his life, Lord."

She had seen the whole thing happening from afar, almost as if in slow-motion. As the terrible scene unfolded before her eyes in all of its horror, she whispered a silent heartfelt prayer. *Dear God, what in the world is happening?* But God did not tell her at that moment. She knew deep in her heart that God was in control, and right now she did not really expect an answer. It was more an outcry of desperation as she saw her friend struggling.

She knew Abe Mortimer well. He had been a personal friend ever since he had turned away from his less than honest ways several years ago, and had joined Pastor Julian's church. Pastor Julian, known affectionately as Papa Julian, had really taken Abe under his wing. "Miss Molly...," Abe had told her with a solemn expression on the day of his baptism, "...from now on, I will walk the straight and narrow. My past is buried and I am a new man."

And he had been true to his words, as he tirelessly gave himself to the many projects of the community, and was soon chosen as a deacon in Papa Julian's church.

And now he was rushing to Greenacre's emergency department as limp as an old dish cloth. The victim of a rogue sponge cake!

Abe had been in excellent health, and could eat like a wolf. As far as Molly could remember, the dear man never had any problems with swallowing food before.

Then again, there's always a first time for everything.

Right next to Molly stood her assistant, Dora Brightside.

Normally she was a great support in the running of the agency. She was sensible, intelligent, sharp and meticulously organized. But not now.

At this moment Dora, dressed in white slacks and a hairy white sweater with black buttons, looked more like a ruffled polar bear than a bright assistant, and her face was as white as the clothes she was wearing. For an instant, Molly even feared Dora would faint. The poor woman seemed in shock as she continually moved her lips without uttering a sound.

Molly pinched her hard in the arm. "Snap out of it, Dora."

It worked. Dora let out a deep sigh and looked with unbelieving eyes at Molly. "Oh, Miss Molly…," she said, "… what a terrible, terrible thing to happen."

Molly Gertrude nodded. It was. A most unfortunate incident, and very strange as well.

The whole place was stunned to an eerie silence, and even though Billy Monroe and Charmayne Mortimer were officially man and wife, nobody wore a smile anymore. This day was ruined.

But all the while, Molly Gertrude kept thinking. Something just didn't sit right. What are the chances of anybody choking on soft creamy cake? Of course, people had died of stranger things before, like the man she'd read about who died of swallowing a fly, but still it was strange. And why had Billy Monroe made that unusual move just before his father-in-law fell over?

He had refused to eat the first bite of cake, insisting Abe Mortimer took the first mouthful. It was a well-known tradition that the bride and the groom would cut the cake together, and then, with the photographer clicking away on his fancy camera, the two love birds would feed each other the first blissful morsels.

But that had *not* happened this time.

After Billy and Charmayne had cut the cake together with a very sharp knife, and everyone was waiting for that golden moment when they would stuff the wedding cake into each other's mouth, getting the gooey stuff all over their faces, Billy had unexpectedly and loudly proclaimed, "Today, I break a tradition out of deep respect for my precious father-in-law."

Huh? What's he up too? Everyone had wondered what he was going to do.

He had turned to his father-in-law and spoken in cheerful tones, "Father... Abe... I want you to eat the cake first, before anyone else does. You deserve it, as you are the best. This is to honor you."

Strange.

Why did he put Abe on the spot like that? Abe had refused at first, and had tried to wave away the piece that Billy held up before him. "No, Billy... The first piece of the wedding cake always needs to be eaten by the bride and the bridegroom."

Billy only shook his head. "No, Abe... The honor is yours." Then he had practically forced the wedding cake on his father-in-law. Only seconds later the poor man was lying on the floor.

Molly Gertrude stared at the scene before her. Billy was holding the wrenching Charmayne, who was wailing and weeping in long, drawn out, hysterical howls, as he unsuccessfully tried to comfort her. At this moment nothing and nobody could offer the poor girl any comfort.

It was then that a chilling thought hit Molly Gertrude.

What if this wasn't an accident? What if somebody had tried to kill Abe Mortimer?

The thought shocked her, and at first she tried to push it out of her mind. Clearly, she was reading too many mystery novels... This had been nothing but an unfortunate accident.

Still, the thought was clear and persistent, and Molly Gertrude had been around long enough to know that when she felt this way about something, she should not just brush it off as nonsense.

Of course it was too early to tell, but Molly Gertrude decided then and there that when Sheriff J.J. Barnes arrived, she would have to tell him to make sure to check the contents of that cake. It *could* have been an accident... but what if it wasn't? That first piece of cake could have been poisoned. If it had, it would be easy to spot and then Billy had some explaining to do. Molly Gertrude noticed that the helpful waiter, apparently trying to be even more helpful, was just throwing away the remains of the broken wine glass in a garbage bag, and was preparing to remove the remains of the cake.

"Nooo!" Molly Gertrude screamed as she ran forward as fast as her old legs could carry her, while she occasionally waved her walking cane in the air.

The waiter saw her coming, threw down the dustpan with the remains of the cake he had collected, jumped up in alarm and began wildly scratching his curly hair. "I-I just wanted to clean up."

"Around a potential crime scene?" Molly Gertrude whispered, giving him a silent scowl. Then she hissed, "Don't touch the cake."

The waiter stared at her with an empty glance and stuttering, "A crime scene? Have you lost your marbles, lady? Sure I'll leave it… as long as I don't get fired for not cleaning up the mess." Clearly he had never been on the scene of an attempted murder before!

The man's cheeks flushed. Molly didn't know if he was embarrassed or angry at her correction, and quite frankly didn't care. Even if she was wrong, which she probably was, she had read enough detective stories to know that nothing should be touched around a the scene of a misdemeanor until the police had given the okay. The waiter scurried away with the garbage bag in hand and tail between his legs.

At that time some sirens were heard in the distance and soon several police cars with blue, flashing lights appeared at the scene.

Sheriff J.J. Barnes had arrived, accompanied by his young assistant, Deputy Sheriff Dawson Digby.

2

MOLLY GERTRUDE AND DORA

*C*almhaven- *June 11*

The day before the wedding

"Still want to come in for a cup of raspberry tea, Dora? I picked up some of your favorite homemade Silky Citrus Curd Cookies last night..." Molly Gertrude cast Dora a sideway glance as she was about to open the door of the car. When Dora arched her brows, Molly Gertrude nodded with her head towards her front door in an inviting way.

"Did you say Silky Citrus Curd Cookies from Tilly's store?" Dora gave Molly Gertrude one of her broad smiles. Her auburn ponytail bobbed with pleasure as she answered. "It's been a long day, Miss Molly, and I am a little tired... but that is an offer I can't refuse." She licked her lips at the prospect of Tilly's homemade delicacies. "I've got not much else planned for the evening anyway."

Molly Gertrude seemed pleased. She opened the door of Dora's second-hand Kia Rio and while she wormed her aging body out of the car she let out a sigh. "Cars were not invented for old people."

Dora chuckled as she turned off the motor. She climbed out herself without much effort and said in a cheerful voice, "Don't complain, Miss Molly. Imagine you would have to walk everywhere by yourself."

Molly Gertrude nodded as she waited for Dora to join her so they could walk together to her front door. "You are right, dear...," she said as she slid her arm around Dora's. "I am a grumpy old lady who is ever so grateful for all you do for me." She looked up into Dora's brown eyes that were peering at her from behind the enormous pink glasses that were perched on her nose. "I couldn't really do it without you, Dora. How long have you actually been helping me with the agency?"

Dora shrugged her shoulders as they walked towards Molly Gertrude's front door. "Next month it will be exactly ten years, I think."

Molly Gertrude stopped at the porch and looked up at Dora with her brows cocked in surprise. The wind was playing with a lock of her short, white hair that was usually kept in immaculate shape by the rollers she had used for at least fifty years. "Has it really been that long? My, oh my... Time sure flies," she snickered. "Ten years ago I was still considering myself a young doe."

Dora giggled, but did not dare to contradict her.

When Dora first started working for Miss Molly Gertrude Grey, the stubborn lady wouldn't use her cane, therefore she tilted when she walked. With much love Dora teased her about tilting and affectionately joked about Molly's stubbornness at times.

After Molly Gertrude had rummaged in her brown leather handbag (the small one that sported the finger-sized glass image of her cat Misty) she found her house key, and seconds later the door swung open with a loud creak.

A small suburban house it was, right on the edge of town in a quiet neighborhood of Calmhaven, and just at the beginning of the vast forest that stretched out all the way to the coast. The house itself was nothing fancy, but it was clean, not too big, and not too small. It had a lovely rose garden in front, a small patio in the back where Molly Gertrude always loved to sit on a warm summer evening, and inside there was a place for everything and everything was in its place. Just the way Molly Gertrude liked it.

Even though Molly Gertrude was certainly aging, she felt age was never an excuse to let things slide, and as long as she could still get up in the mornings she was determined to keep her surroundings clean and well-organized.

"Imagine the Good Lord would show up for a visit," she would often chuckle. "I wouldn't want him to wrinkle his nose and shake his head because I failed to keep my place neat, would I?"

"I guess not," Dora would answer dutifully, and she would invariably wonder if she would be just as perky as Miss Molly when she herself reached such a respectable age.

But the years were beginning to tell on Molly with her wavy, white hair and her endearing smile. In the mornings she was, and these were her own words, as stiff as a dried-out sausage, but in spite of her increasing physical ailments, the little pains and the sometimes not so little pains, she kept the place shiny and in pristine condition. And, truth be told, she had more life and spunk in her than many people half her age.

Of course, for the major jobs in the home she called in outside help. Just recently, Aaron Taylor had renovated the roof of her house for a special price. The roof had begun to leak in a storm and Aaron was called in the very next morning. It took him two full days, but when he was done, he boasted with a grand smile the covering was good again for another fifty years.

"If I make it another ten, I'll be as happy as a lark," Molly Gertrude had chuckled while she had rubbed her wrinkled hands. But she was sure thankful for Aaron's good work, and even more thankful, that she was still able to live by herself with her cat Misty in such a lovely spot at the edge of Calmhaven, surrounded by friends and her ever-growing collection of sleuthing-women books.

After Molly Gertrude had guided Dora into the living room and her assistant had settled into one of the plush, comfortable seats, she walked slowly to the kitchen to get the tea ready and minutes later she joined Dora again with a happy smile, a tray full of cookies and a steaming pot of raspberry tea.

"I am sure glad organizing the wedding is behind us," Molly Gertrude began as she placed the tray with cookies before Dora on the coffee table. "Now all we need to do is make sure everyone does their part. I think the wedding will be a great success tomorrow."

Dora nodded as she picked up one of the cookies. "Everything is ready. The food, the music, the arrangements… nothing is left to chance." As she nibbled on her cookie she leaned back into her seat as a satisfied expression washed over her face.

Tomorrow, Mayor Abe Mortimer's daughter Charmayne was getting married, and Molly Gertrude, the owner of the Cozy Bridal Agency had been hired to make all the necessary arrangements. Both Molly Gertrude and Dora had worked almost non-stop for the last two weeks and now, finally, everything was ready.

"We did it again, Miss Molly."

Molly Gertrude mumbled while slightly nodding her head, to a black and white portrait of a lady in old fashioned clothes that was hanging on the wall above the empty fireplace.

Dora arched her brows. "You actually never told me about that woman. Who is she...your mother, maybe?"

Molly frowned. "I know I am old, Dora, but I am not ancient. That picture was taken in 1875. It's a photograph of my great-geat-great-great-Aunt on my father's side. Can't you tell by her hairstyle?"

Dora let out a soft whistle. "That's very old then, and her name was Molly too?"

"That's right," Molly Gertrude chuckled. "She was Molly Gertrude White the first. I think I am the fifth or sixth Molly Gertrude... I may have lost count somewhere along the line. But, that woman..." she pointed with her finger in the direction of the painting, "... was the founder of the original Cozy Bridal Agency. It all started with her."

"I see," Dora said, and nodded respectfully.

Molly Gertrude leaned forward and poured Dora a cup of steaming hot tea while she narrowed her eyes as if deep in thought. "Have I never told you the history of the agency, in all these ten years?"

"No," Dora shook her head as she picked up another one of Mollie's cookies. "You have not."

"The Cozy Bridal Agency goes a long way back," Molly Gertrude said and her face got a faraway look. "Molly Gertrude White, first founded it, although in those days, I am sure, the agency was quite different from what it is today. She started it right after the Civil War. I suppose people were desperate in those days... You know with husbands killed in the war, women left behind with a slew of kids and lonely men settling the Western frontier. When she started the Cozy Bridal Agency it was an instant success. Her husband was a detective which caused her to become somewhat a sleuth on the side."

"Have you ever heard of Mail Order Brides?"

"No."

"When the men went to settle the West, they were lonely and advertised for women to join them as wives. Molly's Cozy Bridal Agency sent out hundreds of brides. Molly Gertrude White was very careful matching her brides. Periodically she visited her brides to make sure they weren't being mistreated."

Dora smacked her lips. "Things sure have changed since those early days."

"I know," Molly sighed. "Sometimes, I am afraid I can't quite follow it anymore. Nowadays, men and women alike can just go online, find some obscure dating site and before they know it they get themselves in a boat load of trouble." She stirred her tea a little too wildly and spilled some on the coffee table.

"It's called progress, Miss Molly," Dora said with a grin.

Molly Gertrude looked at Dora. She wanted to argue the point, but when she stared at Dora's gentle, smiling brown eyes, hidden behind her enormous pink glasses, she couldn't help but smile back and agree. "You are right,

Dora. It's good that things keep changing. It has helped the agency as well."

"Tell me more," Dora asked. "I suppose, Molly Gertrude the first handed the business over to her daughter, who was also named Molly Gertrude…"

"No she had no children. It was passed within the family, mostly to those girls carrying her name."

"So the agency stayed in the family, and was eventually handed down to you."

Molly Gertrude nodded. "That's right, except my mother was the odd woman out, I should say. She didn't care for a Bridal Agency, and even though she never sold it, she let my aunt run the place." Molly Gertrude chuckled. "My mother just didn't fit. Even her name wasn't Molly Gertrude, but Amelia. When she died I inherited the agency… I took up the torch, and here we are today."

"But you don't have any children, so…" Dora's voice trailed off, "…what will happen to the agency when… well… you know—"

"When I die?" Molly Gertrude interrupted Dora as she peered at her assistant, but her eyes were not unfriendly. "I've made some arrangements." She let out a soft chuckle. "But, I suppose, we'll cross that bridge when we get there, won't we?"

Dora blushed while she had her mouth full of Citrus Curd and shook her head in an effort to apologize. She took a sip of her tea to wash away the remains of the cookie and then said, "You've made the agency into a flourishing business. Ever since you have extended your business and have become an official wedding planner, we've got almost more work than we can handle."

"And that at my age," Molly Gertrude said pensively as she lightly shook her head. "But I have you to thank for that, Dora. I don't know if we would be doing so well if it wasn't for that special organizational talent of yours. Tomorrow, the Cozy Bridal Agency will play a big part again in the happiness of two young people." She lifted her cup of tea in the air as if she were bringing out a toast. "To the happiness of Charmayne Mortimer and Billy Monroe."

Dora lifted her already empty teacup in the air as well, but quickly put it back down on the coffee table and cleared her throat. "Do you really think Billy Monroe is a good match for that tender-hearted Charmayne?"

Molly frowned.

"He seems…," Dora explained, "…how should I say it…" She furrowed her brow and tilted her head a bit to the side. "… a bit shifty maybe, and extremely foolish."

"And you are the expert on relationships?" Molly Gertrude let out a giggle as she narrowed her eyes, but quickly swallowed her giggles as she noticed the hurt expression on Dora's face. "I mean to say," correcting herself, "that it really doesn't matter what we think or don't think. They are two grown-up people and they are making their own decisions." Then she added in a lighter tone, "Of course, you may still object… You know how Papa Julian always says something like, 'If there's anyone who objects to this union, let him speak up now, or forever hold his peace.'" She peered at Dora. "You can still throw a monkey wrench in the whole affair, although I sincerely hope you won't. It wouldn't be a very good advertisement for our agency." Then she frowned and said with suppressed laughter, "But I get it… you were maybe hoping to marry Billy Monroe yourself."

Dora's face flushed. "Me…? Good heavens, no way!" She lowered her eyes and groaned, "As I said, I just have my doubts about Billy. And as for me… I am afraid I will never get married." She let out a deep sigh and stared at the wooden floor of Molly Gertrude's living room.

Molly Gertrude raised her eyebrows. "Why do you say that? You have so much to give… You are still young, pretty and bubbly. I would say you are a real treasure."

Dora cast her a timid smile and mumbled something Molly Gertrude could not understand. Then she leaned over and grabbed another Silky Citrus Curd Cookie.

"What about that young gentleman at the police station?" Molly Gertrude insisted. "What's his name again? Digby?"

"Digby," Dora corrected Molly Gertrude, but as she said his name, Molly Gertrude noticed Dora blushed.

"He seems like a nice young man," Molly Gertrude said as she leaned back. "I would thin—"

"Do you think the wedding cake will turn out all right?" Dora cut Molly Gertrude off and changed the subject forcefully.

"Of course it will. Why do you even ask?"

"Because we've arranged everything, except for the cake. Charmayne and Billy wanted us to take care of even the smallest details, but when I mentioned the cake, Billy was quite adamant, even to the point of being rude. "The wedding cake is none of your business." Dora mimicked Billy's dark voice. "I felt like a schoolgirl being reprimanded for chewing gum."

Molly Gertrude smiled as she looked at Dora, who nervously licked a few obstinate cookie crumbs off her lips. Even though Molly Gertrude had told Dora not to worry about it, it seemed her assistant was still holding a bit of a grudge.

"If their wedding cake is bad, or something is wrong with it, it will reflect negatively on the agency," Dora added.

"Of course it won't, Dora Brightside," Molly Gertrude said in a decisive voice. "Have you not heard who is responsible for the wedding cake? I thought you knew."

Dora gave Molly Gertrude a blank stare.

"The wedding cake is made by Alfred," Molly answered, as she almost whispered the name in respect. "He's the best cake maker in the whole region. His cakes are ten times better than my silly Silky Citrus Curd Cookies."

Dora's face flushed. "I didn't know that."

Molly Gertrude shrugged. "If you marry, and your best man happens to be a fabulous cake maker as well, it's quite normal you ask him to prepare the wedding cake. Wouldn't you do the same?" Molly Gertrude gave Dora an encouraging smile and added, "Wait till you get your hands on that wedding cake. Then, and only then, will you know what they serve the angels in heaven."

Dora pressed her lips together and nodded as she thought about it. Then she wrinkled her nose and she balked, "Still, I don't like Billy Monroe." After she said it, she dropped the subject and a wide grin appeared. "But, you are wrong about one thing…"

"What's that?"

Dora chuckled. "I don't think Albert Finney's cake can be better than your cookies. Nothing, absolutely nothing, can beat those."

Just then Misty jumped on Dora's lap, but it wasn't meant as a show of affection. While purring, she used Dora as a springboard, and only a second later, before the astonished eyes of Dora, she landed with all four paws on the coffee table and began to nibble on the last remaining Citrus Curd cookie.

Dora shook her head. "I thought Misty loved me, but she's only using me to get what she wants." She curled her lips.

"Cats are carnivores, Miss Molly. You shouldn't spoil Misty like that."

"Can't help it," Molly Gertrude chuckled. "I spoil all my friends and that includes you, as I still have a few more cookies left in the kitchen, Dora. Just for you."

3

WAS IT REALLY AN ACCIDENT?

C almhaven, June 12

Right after Abe Mortimer had keeled over

Police inspector John Joseph Barnes, JJ to most of the folks in Calmhaven, was a serious looking police officer. At least, that's how he liked to see himself. Strong, muscled and always in control. And he tried hard to live up to the image he had of himself. He figured such an intimidating presence would be enough to scare people into behaving properly. *Don't mess with JJ Barnes. He's in control.*

And it had worked. At least, that's what he thought. And according to the statistics and his own calculations, there was hardly any crime to speak of in Calmhaven.

JJ Barnes was in control. And it was true that he had a

massive body. His square shoulders and the muscled arms that stuck out of his short-sleeved uniform gave the impression of a seasoned prize-fighter. His equally square face with the sharply chiseled jawbones, the bristly mustache, and the peering eyes matched the picture as well.

But everyone who knew JJ Barnes a bit better, and that was pretty much the whole town, knew that underneath the uniform, there was a jolly man, close to retirement, who was the only perfect candidate in town to dress up like Santa Claus during the holiday season. After all, his body was not only massive, but clearly overweight as well. That was mostly due to his love for a good, cold Budweiser or two. He had gotten into many an argument with his wife about his fast protruding belly, but so far, her gentle words of wisdom had fallen on deaf ears. And the townspeople did not mind as the true nature of JJ Barnes would come out after only a few sips of the celebrated malt and then he would be cracking jokes and looked nothing like a much to be feared officer of the law.

But today he was on duty, and as he stepped into the wedding hall, looking gruff, everyone knew it was best to stay out of his way.

Everyone that is except Molly Gertrude Grey. As soon as she saw the police man enter, followed by Deputy Digby, she staged herself strategically close to the place where Abe Mortimer had tumbled to the ground, apparently waiting for her chance to speak to the man.

"I am sorry for this terrible affair, Miss Mortimer," Barnes mumbled to Charmayne who was still weeping uncontrollably.

Charmayne looked up. "It's Mrs. Monroe," she howled. "I just got married, but thank you anyway."

Barnes' face flushed. "Sorry, Miss... eh Mrs. Can you tell me what happened?"

"Leave her alone, JJ." Best man Albert Finney stepped forward and stared with angry eyes at the policeman. "Can't you see she's distressed? You can talk to us. We all saw what happened here."

Barnes frowned, forcing his eyes into an icy stare. "What *did* happen, Finney?"

"An accident," Finney fired back. "He choked and fell over."

"Dead?"

"Well, we don't know, but he sure looked very unwell!"

"He choked? On what?"

"Cake."

JJ Barnes curled his lips. "You mean he choked on a nut in the cake or something?"

"No, he did not. The nuts in the cake were mashed up. It was a sponge cake."

Barnes pulled on his mustache. "How then can you choke on sponge cake?"

Finney shrugged his shoulders. "I don't know. But it

happened."

"It's true, officer," Charmayne wailed as she looked up at the police man. "We all saw it... he choked and fell over. The medics rushed him to the hospital, and we don't even know if he's alive or d...d..." Another wave of tears rolled in and she turned her face away again.

Barnes pressed his lips together and nodded. "Most unfortunate," he mumbled. "A most unfortunate accident." Then he turned to Digby. "Just take a few statements, Digby, for the record. This was clearly an accident, and this case is as good as closed."

"Excuse me JJ?" A soft, feminine voice behind the police officer caught his attention. He turned and looked into Molly Gertrude Grey's gentle eyes.

"Miss Grey?" Barnes tipped his blue cap with the words 'police' written on it. "I heard what happened. A very unfortunate accident."

"It certainly seems so," Molly answered, "but not everything is always as it seems, Sheriff. At least, isn't it too early to tell?"

"What do you mean?" Barnes barked, narrowing his eyes as he stared at the old lady. He had always tried to like Molly Gertrude Grey, but he couldn't truthfully say he had always succeeded in that mission. Most people liked Molly Gertrude, but he had never been able to fully figure her out. Of course, she was a gentle, old lady, and yes, he liked her... a little, and only on the fringes of his heart.

She was the nosey sort and he didn't like nosey people. She always badgered him about little things that happened in Calmhaven with the famous five W's of journalism. What, Where, Why, Who and When? But because nothing ever really happened in Calmhaven, no doubt due to his own professional presence, there was never anything to satisfy her curiosity, and she apparently filled her appetite for mystery by stuffing her mind full of unrealistic crime novels.

And here she was again, meddling in affairs that were none of her business and he hoped his rough response would put her back in her place.

But Molly Gertrude Grey did not seem intimidated. She cleared her throat and said, "It may very well be an accident, but what if..." she lowered her voice and leaned over to JJ Barnes' ear, "... someone was trying to murder him."

"Murder?" Barnes cried out, stunning the people around. "Why do you think such a thing?"

A shock went through Charmayne's body and she began another round of hysterical wails. "Murder?" she cried out, "Someone was trying to kill daddy?"

"Quiet," JJ Barnes yelled, "Nobody really means that, and we don't even know if he is...well, you know... It's only Miss Molly Gertrude saying it."

Molly Gertrude sighed as she leaned heavily on her cane. "I whispered for a reason, JJ. But all I am aski—"

"We'll take it from here, Miss Grey," Barnes interrupted her. "You are just reading too many Miss Marple books. Sometimes things just happen, and that's it." Without giving Molly Gertrude another glance he turned around and walked away gritting his teeth. *Maybe it was time for that old lady to move away from Calmhaven. After all, there's a good nursing home only 20 miles further down in Tapiano.*

Billy had taken Charmayne in his arms and tried to gently move her away from the scene while his wife was still sobbing. Barnes took off his cap as they brushed by. "Sorry, Mr. Monroe," he whispered. "I am very sorry for your distress, young lady."

In passing Billy gave him a quick glance. There were tears in his eyes too, and Barnes felt a pang of pain. How sad and what a tragic thing to happen on your wedding day. This was truly a horrible day for everyone involved.

As Barnes stared after the heartbroken newlyweds he was certain, no matter what Molly Gertrude Grey insinuated, this was nothing more than a most unfortunate accident.

JJ Barnes had made it painstakingly clear that he wasn't about to consider any other option, but Molly Gertrude wasn't willing to be easily fobbed off. Sure, it was possible she was wrong, but how much better to be wrong and get everybody upset, than to be right and not do anything about it, so that a would-be killer would go free. What's more, she noticed a burning sensation troubling her left shoulder. She had not felt that peculiar itch for quite some time, but it always seemed to appear on moments when something was amiss; when people were lying, or someone was covering up something. Only a fleeting sensation of course, and not something that would dazzle the police, but still it was enough to make Molly Gertrude decide she needed to do some sniffing around.

As soon as JJ had so rudely turned around and walked off, she spotted Deputy Digby. The blond haired, skinny policeman with his timid smile and baby-blue eyes had always respected her, and if JJ wouldn't listen, maybe Digby would.

Full of determination Molly Gertrude strode to the deputy, who had just finished taking Billy Monroe's statement.

"Check that cake, Digby," she said as she approached the man, while waving her finger in the direction of the cake. "It may very well have been an accident, but check-that-cake." She articulated the words deliberately.

Digby looked up from his notepad and when he heard what Molly Gertrude had said, he began to scratch his blond hair under his police cap with his pen. For a moment he stared with big, round eyes at Molly Gertrude. "Why, Miss Grey?"

"I hope I am wrong, but something smells fishy here."

Digby gave her a blank stare. "I don't smell anything, Miss Grey…"

Molly Gertrude shook her head. "I mean, Digby, what if that cake was poisoned?"

The man's face paled. "You believe the cake was poisoned? But it was an accident, wasn't it?"

Molly pressed her lips together. "We will never know unless you take it to the laboratory. Isn't it common sense to get all the facts straight when somebody may have died? We can't just *assume* the poor man suffered asphyxiation. We need to be certain."

Digby frowned. "I'll check with my boss."

"Don't," Molly said, more forceful than she wanted. "He as good as said the case is closed…" The man licked his lips and hesitated.

"Please, Digby…" Molly put on her sweetest smile. "Just do it for me… as a favor."

Digby tilted his head. "But if I…"

"The lab will be happy to have something to do," Molly insisted.

Digby's face brightened. "Alright, Miss Grey. I'll scoop up some of the cake and bring it to the lab."

Molly smiled, glad this victory was won. "Be sure to take some of the stuff that was on his plate, will you Digby? I am mostly interested about the stuff that went into his mouth."

Digby nodded. "Consider it done, Miss Molly."

4

STRANGE DISCOVERIES

Molly Gertrude had just been filling up Misty's saucer with milk and stared pensively at her furry friend, who was greedily licking up the white cream, when the doorbell rang. A timid, short ring it was, and Molly Gertrude raised her brows. She did not expect anyone this early. A glance at the old-fashioned wall-clock told her it was barely 9.00 in the morning.

"Coming," she called out, as she grabbed hold of her walking cane and waddled towards the door. When she peered through the peephole, she raised her brows, as there, looking vulnerable and forlorn was the silhouette of Charmayne Mortimer Monroe.

"Charmayne?" she sputtered, "What a surprise."

Charmayne's eyes were puffy and red, and Molly Gertrude understood. That poor girl's life had been turned upside down. Most likely Charmayne had not slept very well, and that was not because of her wedding night.

"May I come in, Miss Grey?" Her voice was barely audible.

"Of course, dear." Molly Gertrude opened the door wide and made room for her.

No sooner had Charmayne sunk into the seat Molly Gertrude always reserved for visitors, she let out a sob, and stared with watery eyes at Molly Gertrude. Her glance was a strange mixture of emotions. Fear, grief, pain, and Molly Gertrude even sensed a little anger.

For a moment Molly Gertrude feared Charmayne was about to blame her for the whole unfortunate affair; for allowing someone else to have made that cake, or for another yet to be disclosed reason. But when Charmayne started to talk, Molly Gertrude understood.

"Have you heard from the hospital, dear?"

"Yes, Daddy is breathing, thank the good Lord, but he is still in a coma."

"Oh, my dear. What a relief he is not…"

Molly could not bear to say the word.

"Dead," Charmayne completed Molly's sentence.

"I believe…," she asserted in a soft, but decisive voice, "… Someone tried to kill Daddy. And the police do *not* believe it."

Molly Gertrude arched her brows as she sat down next to Charmayne. "What makes you say that?" she asked, trying to sound as objective as possible, but she pricked up her ears. Apparently Charmayne did not believe it had been an accident either.

"Several things," Charmayne wailed as she opened her handbag. She took out a handkerchief to clear the tears from her eyes. "Of course…," she began hesitantly, "… it's technically possible to get food in the air passage and choke, still, I really wonder if that is what happened." She looked up and Molly Gertrude could sense deep, unresolved grief. "My Daddy was strong as a bear, and he never gobbled up his food. He always told me not to swallow stuff too soon. That's because of what happened to my aunt."

"Oh?" Molly Gertrude vacillated. "What happened to her?"

"You didn't know?" Charmayne went on. "My aunt suffocated. I was only ten years old when she choked on a chicken bone… and it was very different from the way Daddy choked." Her words came out in a depressing tone.

Molly Gertrude frowned. "In what way was it was different?"

"I'll never forget the desperate expression on my aunt's face as she was trying to get air," Charmayne moaned. "First she was coughing and wheezing. Then she grabbed her throat and her lips turned blue, but it soon spread to her face. Help came too late."

Molly Gertrude scooted closer in order to grab the girl's hands.

"But the way Daddy acted was very different. His face was flushed, but he did not turn blue. Never." Charmayne now blubbered out the words. "Instead of his throat, he grabbed his chest, as if a sharp pain jabbed him, and even though he was coughing and wheezing, it just didn't sound the same as when my aunt died."

Molly Gertrude's chest was aching. It always did when she wanted to help someone, but there was nothing she *could* do. "I am so sorry you had to witness these events, Charmayne."

Charmayne pushed her tears away and pressed her lips together so hard they turned white. "I just know Daddy didn't choke on his cake."

Molly thought for a moment. "Could he have had heart failure?"

Charmayne shrugged. "It happens. I've heard about people who suddenly fall over when their heart stops, but as I said already, Daddy's health was excellent. He didn't smoke, he barely drank alcohol, and even though he was well into his seventies, he still attended the gym three or four times a week." She let out a frustrated sigh. "I asked Sheriff JJ Barnes about it…"

"And?"

"He said he would look into it, but I had the feeling I was

annoying him. He did not seem very eager to investigate... That's why I came to you, Miss Grey."

Molly Gertrude leaned back. "I don't understand."

Charmayne let out a deep sigh. "JJ Barnes, no doubt, is a good man, but I think too many years as an officer has left him tired and cynical. He's thinking in terms of expenses and keeping up appearances. For him it's much more convenient to simply accept it was an accident..." She hesitated, but then her eyes lit up, "...but you yourself mentioned it, yesterday, that it could have been a murder." She peered questioningly at Molly Gertrude. "You *did* say that, didn't you?"

Molly Gertrude cleared her throat. "Yes, I did say that, Charmayne. But, I must be fair, it still could have been an accident. It's too early to tell, but I must confess, I have my doubts too. I asked Officer Digby to take the cake to the laboratory, just to see if it was poisoned."

Charmayne gasped. "The cake? But Billy gave it to him... You don't mean to say that Billy..." Her voice trailed off, and she never finished her sentence.

"I am not saying anything at all," Molly Gertrude clarified. "If that cake turns out to be poisoned, *anybody* could have messed with it, not just Billy." She narrowed her eyes. "How is Billy doing, anyway? It must have been a great shock to him as well."

Charmayne shrugged her shoulders. "He seems pretty aloof about it. I scolded him for it this morning. He just answered not to get too uptight, and that bad things just happen in this world."

Insensitive fellow. Molly Gertrude remembered how Dora had mentioned she thought Billy was not a good match for Charmayne, as she felt the bridegroom was shallow and shifty.

"If someone would have wanted to murder your father, who comes to mind, and why?" Molly Gertrude chided herself for sounding so calculating and formal, but she *had* to ask the question.

Charmayne rubbed her forehead. "You know Daddy wasn't always the good Christian man he was since he joined Papa Julian's church, right?"

Molly Gertrude nodded. She knew all too well. Abe Mortimer had been a shrewd businessman when Charmayne was still a toddler, with little regard for the law or his fellow man. Whenever the subject of his dark past came up, he would press his lips together and say he had fallen into the trap of the deceitfulness of riches.

In those days, it was even whispered he had strong ties to the underworld. Abe himself never admitted to it, although he never denied it either. But then his life changed. He found God and a remarkable change came over him. Much like the wee little man Zaccheus, the tax-collector in the days of Jesus, Abe's heart was touched, and he too went through great lengths of repaying everyone he had defrauded. That's when he got baptized and joined Papa Julian's church. Molly and he became best of friends there, but his troubles were not all over. Charmayne's mother, Isabelle, did not take Abe's new found faith very kindly and refused to go along with it. At first she mocked him, then started to call him all kinds of unsavory names, and when she finally began to hurl pottery at Abe's head, Abe knew he had to draw the line somewhere. He sold their house, gave most of the money to Isabelle and tried to start a new life. Isabelle, who apparently was only interested in his money, then ran off with her personal trainer from the gym, a man 20 years her junior. Neither Abe, nor Charmayne ever heard from her again.

"Does anyone come to mind that could have done such a dreadful thing?" Molly Gertrude asked again.

New tears formed in Charmayne's eyes. Then she shook her head. "I wish I knew... but I don't. But the main reason I think of foul play is this..." She stuck her hand in her handbag again and pulled out a wrinkled sheet of paper.

"What is it?" Molly Gertrude asked as she tilted her head in surprise.

"I found this a week ago in my father's bedroom." She handed the paper to Molly Gertrude, who unfolded it. "I had wanted to ask Daddy about it, but you know, with the wedding and all... I just kept postponing it."

As Molly Gertrude stared at the paper, her heart skipped a beat. On the paper, with letters that were cut out of a newspaper was a small and chilling message:

Stay out of my life, or else...

Molly Gertrude felt the blood rising to her head. "And you found this a week ago?"

Charmayne nodded.

"Where exactly did you find it?"

Charmayne pressed her lips together. "I am not one for snooping around in my Daddy's bedroom. I had no reason to, but I was looking for my mother's pearly collier. I thought my Daddy still had it, and it would have looked so nice with my wedding dress."

"And...?"

Charmayne shrugged her shoulders. "I should have waited for my Daddy to return, but I couldn't wait and I went into his room. I found it in the drawer of his desk."

"Maybe it was an old message?" Molly Gertrude suggested, although she knew that wasn't true. Still she had to ask to rule out that possibility. "You know something from his former life that he somehow kept."

Charmayne shook her head. "No, Miss Grey. This paper is not old." She took it out of Molly's hand and brought it to her nose. "Smell it. It's fresh and recent, and it was on top of his ledger that he keeps his records in for this year. No, he received this letter recently."

Molly Gertrude fell back in her seat. "I've had that strange burning sensation again in my shoulder, you know."

Charmayne stared at her, not understanding.

"I mean to say I agree with you, Charmayne. I doubt that it was an accident as well, Charmayne," Molly gritted her teeth. "I believe it's been foul play indeed."

At that instant the old rotary phone, standing on a small table in the corner, started to ring, loud and demanding. It shook both women up as none of them had expected it.

Dora had often tried to sell Molly Gertrude on the idea of a smartphone, but Molly Gertrude, being the old-fashioned lady she was, still swore by an antique phone and preferred a device with a dial that you needed to turn with your fingers.

"Excuse me, dear," she said as she got up, lumbered to the phone and picked up the horn.

"Hello," she said when she had positioned the horn against her good ear, "you are speaking with the Molly Gertrude Grey. Who is calling?"

For a moment it was still, as Molly Gertrude listened to the voice on the other end. Then she smiled broadly. "Officer Digby, you are early…"

She was still again, let out a few uh's and ahem's, and then grimaced. "Really? Is that so?" At last, she wrinkled her nose, mumbled a word of thanks, and after she said goodbye, she placed the horn back on the hook with a sigh.

"Good news?" Charmayne queried.

"The cake..." Molly began.

Charmayne's eyes widened. "What about it?"

"The results came back from the laboratory."

"And?"

"Nothing. The cake was good. Not a trace of poison. Just the regular stuff you put in a cake, sugar, cream. Nothing out of the ordinary." Molly sighed. "JJ Barnes has officially closed the investigation."

Charmayne's nostrils flared. "What about an autopsy?"

Molly Gertrude thought for a moment. "I'll talk to JJ Barnes about the warning letter you found."

Charmayne did not seem pleased. "I don't like JJ Barnes," she grumbled. Then she looked up with pleading eyes, "Please, Miss Grey... will you look around too. Even if JJ Barnes opens the investigation again, still I'd feel much better if you looked into it as well. Will you please help me to find out what really happened?"

As Molly Gertrude looked at the fragile, broken girl in the chair next to her there was only one thing she could answer. "Yes, Charmayne. I will."

"There's one more thing, Miss Grey."

"What?"

"It's probably nothing, but I also found Daddy's diary." She pulled out a small book with a brown, leather cover and a silk book marker. "I started to read it, but I had to stop. It's just too personal, and it makes me feel so sad. But maybe there's something in there that may help you. After all, you look at everything with objective eyes."

Molly Gertrude nodded. She felt Charmayne's pain, and wished she could take it away, but she couldn't. All she could do was her best to find out what had happened to Charmayne's Daddy. "Thank you, Charmayne... I'll do what I can."

Charmayne nodded in thanks.

"Dora and I will get to work," Molly Gertrude continued. "Whatever happened, we will get the truth on the table."

5

AN ANNOYING LITTLE, OLD LADY

"What can I do for you?" JJ Barnes did not look up when Molly Gertrude entered his office early the next morning, but kept on reading a report, while marking a passage with his yellow highlighter. "I am a little busy."

"Good morning, Sheriff," Molly Gertrude said in as sweet a voice as she could muster. "Thank you for seeing me."

Barnes looked up impatiently. "We are here to serve the people, so if someone wants to see me…, well, they can. What's wrong this time, Molly?"

Molly Gertrude licked her lips. Barnes was not in a good mood. "I heard you have officially closed the investigation of Abe Mortimer's unfortunate accident?"

Barnes threw his marker down on the desk and leaned back in his swivel chair. The chair made a loud creak under the weight of the sturdy policeman. The Sheriff curled his lips and hissed, "I have already told you yesterday you shouldn't be reading so many crime novels. Do I have to spell it out for you?" His tone was haughty and Molly Gertrude had to force herself to keep a friendly smile glued on her face.

"There-has-not-been-a-crime," he said in slow, deliberate words. "This case couldn't be any clearer." He lifted his finger in the air and shook it around as if he was the schoolmaster having to deal with a naughty schoolgirl. "Do you have any idea how much it costs to run a full-scale investigation?"

Molly Gertrude shook her head.

"I thought so," Barnes nodded. "But let me tell you, Miss Grey, with all the economic cuts I have had to deal with, and with the stress of keeping this office afloat, I cannot afford to go on some wild goose chase just because your bunions are itching."

Molly Gertrude seemed not impressed. "I understand your difficulties, Sheriff, but Charmayne Mortimer came to me yesterday. She too has her doubts as to how her Daddy ended up in the hospital."

Barnes leaned forward again, still waving his finger around. "Of course, she does. She's heartbroken and…" he hesitated, "… I may add, a little hysterical."

"I heard there were no traces of poison in the cake…" Molly went on.

Barnes' eyes flashed. "That's right, Miss Grey, there were

no traces of poison. We even took samples of Abe Mortimer's saliva and found nothing out of the ordinary. Just sugar, cream, alcohol, and a bit of aspirin. The man was probably trying to conquer a headache, as I've been told he had already been drinking more than was good for him." He arched his brows. "Does that satisfy you, Miss Grey?"

Molly Gertrude could sense the man was getting a little angry, but before she could respond, he added, "And... next time I would appreciate it if you do not order my deputy around. I could have told you even without getting the lab involved that the cake was not poisoned. Police work is just not your business. But it is mine, and, unlike you, I am highly trained."

"I am sorry, Sheriff," Molly Gertrude replied in a soft voice. Aggravating the man more would do more harm than good. "I did not mean to get you upset."

"Good," Sheriff Barnes grumbled. "Then that settles the matter. Anything else?"

Molly hesitated. At last she opened her purse and pulled out the message that Charmayne had given her. "What do you make of this, Sheriff?" She placed the paper over Barnes' report, right under his nose.

"What is that?" Barnes curled his lip but after he had read it, his face took on a confused expressed. "Where did you get that?"

"Charmayne Mortimer found it in her father's bedroom, only a few days ago."

Barnes stared at the paper, then shook his head, and snorted. "It's not enough to start an investigation."

Molly Gertrude tilted her head to the side. "Why not? That is a serious threat. Who would write such thing and then a couple days later, poor Abe is in a coma?"

Barnes shook his head. "I don't know. A prank maybe, a joke? Witnesses told me that everyone thought Abe Mortimer was just joking when he actually choked. 'Typically one of Billy Monroe's classic, stupid jokes.' Maybe this was a joke too."

Molly Gertrude shook her head. "I don't mean to contradict you, Sheriff, but as you well know, Abe's choking *wasn't* a joke. You can't just assume this threat is a joke. What if there's a would-be-killer out there?"

Sheriff Barnes threw out his arm in exasperation. "There's *no* killer out there, Miss Grey! Who in the world would want to kill Abe Mortimer, anyway? Everybody liked him." His voice jumped from soft to loud. "As you know, I am not much of a churchgoer, but if there was ever a man who 'walked the talk, as you folks say, it was Abe Mortimer. He was always helping people."

Molly Gertrude nodded. "That's why I am so concerned we do not make mistakes."

Sheriff Barnes mumbled something under his breath and sighed. "Even if I wanted to do something, it's not all that easy. As you may well know, we are a very small police force and other than Digby, I've got no one to help me. Besides, I've got other priorities."

Like rescuing cats out of trees, and writing out speeding tickets. "I understand, Sheriff." Molly Gertrude managed to croak.

"Good," Barnes said as he folded his hands and forced a smile on his face. He stared for a moment at the old woman before him. Then his glance softened somewhat, and it seemed an idea had formed in his mind. "Listen, Miss Grey, I will make a deal with you."

"A deal?"

"Sure," Barnes exclaimed. "I have been a little cross with you, and I must say, for good reason. But if you can come up with some real, substantial evidence that this wasn't an accident, I will reopen this case."

Molly raised her brows. "Really?"

"Yes, Miss Grey, *really*," he affirmed, a little annoyed. "And if you now will excuse me, I've got reports to write. Good day, Miss Grey." He picked up his marker again, and stuck his nose back into the form he was working on. The conversation was over.

"Have a good day, Sheriff," Molly Gertrude clipped as she turned around. When she pulled the door closed behind her she thought she heard Sheriff Barnes heaving a great sigh of relief.

❧

Dora's eyes lit up when Molly Gertrude told her about her encounter with Sheriff Barnes. "He said he would reopen the case if you can find evidence of foul play?" She cast Molly an admiring glance. "Then, you are as good as a real detective…"

Molly Gertrude shrugged her shoulders. "Not really Dora. Barnes doesn't actually believe there was foul play involved. He just said that to get rid of me."

"Doesn't matter," Dora quipped. "We can still do some serious investigating." As she thought about it, she tilted her head. "But what did Barnes say when you confronted him with that accusing threat Charmayne found in her Daddy's room? That's something you can't take too lightly."

Molly Gertrude smacked her lips. "He glossed over it. And, in a way, judging from his standpoint, he's right. There really isn't a whole lot to go on, except for our gut feeling that something is wrong."

"Of course he's not right," Dora argued. "He's the police. It's his job to make sure everyone in Calmhaven is safe." When Molly Gertrude did not answer, Dora raised her brows and gasped, "Don't tell me you think we are barking up the wrong tree. You don't really believe it was an accident?" Dora sounded disappointed.

Molly Gertrude shook her head. "No, Dora, I don't think so. I have been wrong about a lot of things in my life, but I don't believe I am wrong about this." She cast Dora a warm smile. "I am personally convinced Abe Mortimer was targeted in some way, by whom and why I do not know. But we need to tread carefully. We just need to find the clue, and believe me, there's always a clue. Always."

"So where do we start?"

"We talk," Molly Gertrude said. "I would like to talk to Albert Finney."

"To Finney? You mean the cake maker?"

"That's right," Molly Gertrude nodded. "We've got to start somewhere. *Somebody* wrote that threat to Abe Mortimer, and if we open our ears we can find out a lot. After all, nobody will suspect two ladies from the Cozy Bridal Agency would be snooping around." Molly Gertrude squeezed her chin with her finger. "Dora, would you want to drive me over to his place?

"Sure," Dora affirmed. "When?"

"I'll give him a call, and I'll ask him when we can come by."

Dora couldn't suppress a chuckle. "This is so exciting. Let's go for it, Miss Molly, and see if we can find out what really happened."

Molly Gertrude frowned. "It's not a game, Dora. If someone tried to kill Abe Mortimer, we are dealing with some very wicked people. You better not forget that."

"Sorry," Dora said in an apologizing tone. "I am ready, whenever you are."

6

FINNEY SHEDS HIS LIGHT ON THE CASE

"**A**lbert Finney... you made the most amazing wedding cake I think I've ever seen in my whole life," Molly Gertrude marveled as she nodded enthusiastically at best man, Finney, who sat opposite her and Dora on a two-seater in his plush living room.

"Thank you," Finney mumbled politely, but Molly Gertrude did not get the impression the man really meant it.

When Molly Gertrude had called him earlier, he had reluctantly agreed to see her and her associate. "Why do you need to see me?" he had asked, his voice less than friendly and much reserved.

"Sorry, Mr. Finney," Molly Gertrude insisted," but the Cozy Bridal Agency was in charge of yesterday's wedding and there are still a few loose ends to take care of."

"When?" Finney had barked through the phone.

Molly Gertrude had answered she and Dora could be there in an hour, he had consented, and hung up. And now they were seated in Finney's richly decorated living room.

Finney, a balding chubby man with meaty jowls that were framed by sideburns in desperate need of a good trim, was sipping a glass of red wine, and peered with dark, shifty eyes through the small, black spectacles that were dancing on his hawk like nose. He had offered the ladies a glass of wine as well, but they had graciously declined. Finney, not wanting to appear inhospitable, had placed a crystal pitcher filled with tap water before them and two glass cups.

"So... what's your business?" he asked, not trying to hide his discomfort as he stared at Molly Gertrude and Dora. "I am sure it's not about my cakes."

Molly Gertrude gave him an endearing smile. "Well, Mr. Finney... it actually is."

The man raised his brows.

"As you know, I am a wedding planner, but one thing that I hardly ever get right is coming up with a good wedding cake." Molly Gertrude leaned a bit forward. "After I saw your cake I was thinking your expertise could be useful in the future."

Surprise flashed over Finney's face and he seemed to relax. "You are here to discuss business?"

"Maybe," Molly Gertrude replied cryptically. "What all was in the cake?"

Finney's face darkened again. "Why do you want to know? I am not about to share my secrets, and certainly not with two wedding planners."

Molly Gertrude giggled. "Don't worry, Mr. Finney. I am not here to steal your secrets. *Actually, I am, but not those relating to your cake.* "To be frank," she continued, "your wedding cake was the best cake I've seen in a long time. Three tiers and the details just right, down to the tiniest chocolate sprinkle…"

Finney relaxed again and a smug expression covered his round face. He nodded. "I am pretty good," he boasted. "My cakes are always good."

"Except…," Molly Gertrude went on, "…somebody almost died eating it."

Gone was the smug expression on Finney's face. He narrowed his beady, little eyes into tiny slits and put his glass of wine down on the coffee table with a loud thud. "And you blame my cake?" he hissed. "How dare you insinuate such a horrible thing! My cakes are soft and spongy. This was the first time in over forty years that somebody choked in the presence of my culinary masterpiece."

Molly Gertrude raised her arms in an apologetic manner. "Sorry, Mr. Finney… please calm down. We are just trying to find out if there was anything that could have triggered this tragedy. As wedding planners it's our responsibility to rule out each and every possible obstacle."

Finney nodded and wanted to say something, but he was interrupted by the ringtone of the mobile phone in his pocket that blared a popular country tune from Dolly Parton. "Excuse me ladies," he said as he fished out his phone. After he glanced at the screen he got up and apologized again. "Sorry, ladies... I'll just have to take this call." He got up and moved away into his kitchen, not wanting Molly Gertrude and Dora to overhear his conversation.

For a moment Molly Gertrude and Dora sat in silence, but then Molly Gertrude's eyes fell onto Finney's wallet, lying right before Dora on the coffee table.

"Look," Molly Gertrude whispered to Dora.

"What?"

"His wallet...," Molly Gertrude spoke barely audible. "It's right before your nose."

Dora frowned. "So?"

"Open it... Take a quick look."

Dora's face changed to unbelief. "B-But that's not proper."

"I know," Molly Gertrude replied, "... and neither is trying to kill Abe Mortimer." She sighed, and forced herself up out of the chair. "I'll do it. We can't always play nice when you have to fight the devil." Dora's mouth hung open as she stared wide-eyed at Molly Gertrude.

"But Finney may not have anything to do with the whole thing?"

Molly Gertrude nodded. "That's why we need to snoop around, so we'll know." She picked up the wallet.

"Hurry, hurry," Dora whispered, barely able to contain her nerves. "He'll be back soon."

But Finney took his time. Both women could hear his muffled voice coming from the kitchen, and Molly Gertrude flicked the wallet open. There was nothing out of the ordinary. Two different credit cards, a pass for the local library... his driver's license...

"For heaven's sake," Dora hissed, "hurry, Miss Molly!"

Molly Gertrude zipped open another small compartment, and fished out a few photographs. A few pictures of an enormous chocolate cake, and two old people... Nobody they knew. Probably his parents. Molly Gertrude was just about to put the pictures back when she spotted a small photograph stuck to the back of the picture of the old people. She took it out and as she stared at it her eyes grew wide. It was a picture of Charmayne. A few years younger, but it was Charmayne all right. As Molly Gertrude turned it over, she read the words *To you my love,* written with red ink and a big red heart was drawn around it.

To you my love? Why would the cake maker be walking around with a picture of Billy's new wife? That was certainly something to muse over.

They could hear Finney's voice, clear and decisive coming from the kitchen. "Thank you for telling me. I'll make sure to look into it. Bye then…"

"He's coming back, Miss Molly…" Dora bit her lips and her hands trembled. "Hurry… please."

Molly Gertrude pushed the picture back into its place, threw the wallet back on the coffee table and just as Finney re-entered the living room she was walking back to her seat. Finney stared at her with a questioning gaze.

"Your garden is lovely," Molly Gertrude said, not knowing what else to say as an explanation of why she was standing up. It wasn't a total lie ether. Finney did have a gorgeous garden, full of rosebushes and a lawn that would make even a man like Tiger Woods a little jealous. Molly Gertrude was standing in front of the giant, glassy, sliding doors, and pointed to a family of sparrows that had landed on the stone porch, hoping to catch a few crumbs.

"You've got a bit of heaven right here, Mr. Finney."

Finney gave her a pleased nod. "Thank you," he said. "Gardens and cakes are the only two passions I have."

And Charmayne Mortimer, maybe? But Molly Gertrude did not say it. Instead she sank back into her seat and took a sip of her water.

"So, Miss Grey," Finney began and a slight smile appeared on his face. He seemed more relaxed, but Molly Gertrude couldn't figure out if it was because of her comments on his garden, or if it was because of the phone call he had just received. "You want to hire me as a cake maker?"

Molly Gertrude tilted her head. "Maybe. I've always heard you made fabulous cakes, but I never actually had the privilege of seeing one, first hand. I am impressed. That's why Dora and I wanted to get to know you a little better."

Finney was now totally at ease. He finished his wine and got up to serve himself another glass. "Are you sure I cannot tempt you with a Carbernet Sauvignon from 2006?"

"I am sure," Molly Gertrude answered also for Dora.

"What a shame your cake got destroyed like that, yesterday," Dora ventured.

Finney nodded. "It sure was. I've been working on that cake for two full weeks, and I haven't gotten paid yet. Now that the old man out of the picture, I can probably say goodbye to my money. After all, whose gonna pay for the cake that caused a catastrophe?"

"Oh? Why is that?" Molly Gertrude's left eyebrow went up.

"That Billy Monroe... He's no good. He's a shifty fellow, very self-centered, and if he had a chance, he would likely even sell his own mother."

"He would?" Molly Gertrude took another sip of her water. "But you were the best man at the wedding?"

A sly smile appeared around Finney's lips. "Billy's no good

for Charmayne." Finney leaned forward and lowered his voice. "Did you know he's got a past?" Another abundant gulp of Cabernet Sauvignon disappeared into Finney's throat. Good. The man was clearly beginning to feel the lubricating effects of the drink.

"Don't we all have a past, Mr. Finney?" Molly Gertrude answered while her face held an innocent, sheepish shine.

"Not like that, Miss Grey." Finney shook his head. "Billy Monroe *really* has a past. He's got a record."

"Oh?"

Finney gave her an enthusiastic nod. "At first, when I was a kid, Billy and I were friends when we attended Calmhaven Elementary School. Of course, I could already sense his dishonesty." Finney shook his head in disgust. "Imagine that. When I was six years old, he stole a whole bag of marbles from me and claimed I had lost them in the river." He let out a chuckle. "I am still mad at him for doing that." He sloshed the wine around in his mouth as he relived Billy's antics. "You know there are marbles and there are really *good* marbles. I, of course, had the really good ones."

Molly Gertrude and Dora both nodded politely.

"But then, when we got older, he really went off the rails. His business failed, and eventually he ended up in jail."

"Did you know Billy still has debts?" Finney lowered his voice to a whisper,

Molly Gertrude didn't know that, and mumbled, "Really?"

"He does. Lots of debts."

"Who to?"

Finney leaned back. "I am not at liberty to say, but trust me, he's got them. You know..." he said, as he waved his index finger up and down, "... it's mighty handy for Billy that his father-in-law happened to choke on my cake... if you get my drift. If the old man kicks the bucket it could lead to a mighty fine payday for Billy-boy." His eyes took on a snake-like appearance.

"You mean..." Molly Gertrude hardly dared to say it, "... because of the inheritance?"

"Smart lady," Finney said, "but you did not hear this from me. I never liked Billy and his criminal past. I preferred to stay friends with Abe Mortimer," Finney added.

"But Abe has a past too," Molly Gertrude interjected.

"That's right," Finney agreed, "but Abe claimed he found God, and that seems to have helped." He smacked his lips. "It's a dumb story of course, since there is no God, but Abe at least became honest. That's why agreed to be best man and make the cake. Sure, Billy and I were old buddies, but Abe, well, let's just say, he was good to me."

Molly Gertrude squeezed her chin with her fingers. "What about Billy? Didn't he join Pastor Julian's church as well?"

Finney couldn't resist a laugh. "He did, but it's all fake.

He's as religious as my neighbor's dog," he scoffed. "That animal acts docile and sweet, but when he gets a chance he always jumps the fence and does his number two in my garden. I am going to shoot that mongrel one of these days."

"And what about your relationship with Charmayne Mortimer?" Molly Gertrude knew she was stepping onto thin ice.

For just a second Finney blushed. Just long enough for Molly Gertrude to notice it, but then his face hardened and he glared at Molly Gertrude. "What kind of question is that?"

Molly Gertrude shrugged and took another sip of her water. "Sorry, it was just a question."

"And a curious one," Finney smirked. "But to answer it, I don't really know her. I was a good friend of Abe's, so he often told me about her woes and troubles. She's a troubled girl and I, being the helpful man that I am, always politely listened. But I have no relationship with Charmayne. I made that cake only out of respect for my friend Abe."

"And now he's confined in a hospital bed, fighting for his life," Molly Gertrude added.

Finney tilted his head and stared at her while he wrinkled his nose. "I am aware of that Miss Grey."

Molly Gertrude didn't like this pompous cake maker. Maybe the man was right about Billy and his shady past, but she wouldn't be surprised if a few cockroaches showed up if the right stones were to be turned around in Finney's heart as well. Thus, she ventured for her last question.

"You don't seem too broken up about your good friend Abe's misfortune?" She almost expected the man to grow angry but instead, a stony expression appeared on his face. He licked his lips and answered in a dark voice, "Problems come to us all, Miss Grey. That is something you yourself will soon experience." He shook his head in clear disgust. "Tell me, why would I mourn for someone else's woes? I have plenty of my own!? It's just nature. Everybody dies someday, sooner or later, and don't give me that tommyrot that Abe's destined for a better place. There's no such thing as a better place."

Molly Gertrude leaned back, almost too stunned to say anything. She noticed Dora was shifting uneasily on her chair as well.

"I sense you don't believe in God?" Molly Gertrude finally asked.

"Of course not," Finney mocked. "This life is all we are ever going to get, and since there's no such thing as *a grand plan...*" he lifted both of his hands in the fashion Papa Julian usually did during his Sunday service, "...I do not see the need to cry when somebody's ready to return to the worms and become fertilizer."

"A most disturbing world view," Molly Gertrude managed to say while she placed her empty water glass back on the coffee table. "I think we are done here." She turned to Dora. "Dora? Ready to go?"

Dora nodded, gulping down her water too, and got up.

"Thank you for your time, Mr. Finney," Molly Gertrude said as she stuck out her hand in order to say goodbye.

Finney didn't take her hand. Instead, another mocking smile appeared on his round face. "I suppose, I won't be making cakes for you in the future then?"

"Who knows," Molly Gertrude said, trying to be polite.

"Don't bother, lady. I've got enough work as it is. After all, I am the best cake maker in this part of the world."

"Good day, Mr. Finney." Without waiting for a response, Molly Gertrude turned around and walked out the door, closely followed by Dora.

7

PAPA JULIAN

The next morning Molly Gertrude and Dora visited Papa Julian, the fatherly pastor of Calmhaven Trinity Church. And for good reason. The encounter with Albert Finney had been anything but pleasant, and Molly Gertrude wanted to see Papa Julian as much for a bit of spiritual relief, as for getting a better idea about the background story on all those involved.

Papa Julian had been Calmhaven's pastor for as long as Molly Gertrude could remember. He had not always carried the title of 'Papa,' neither was such a title official, but he had just sort of grown into it. At first he had been Reverend Julian, or Pastor Julian, while others, mostly those who had no affinity with the church, called him simply by his real name, Julian Maxwell, but even the most unbelieving person in Calmhaven had to admit, the man had a beautiful fatherly heart for people, and somehow everyone just started to call him Papa Julian.

The pastor was a jovial man, with happy, darting brown eyes, and a fringe of white hair around his balding head. His dark brown face always framed a bright white smile for any who came to the door of the church. Julian's lively preaching and passionate faith was infectious, and during his time as pastor in Calmhaven many a soul had been gloriously converted.

But Molly Gertrude and Dora did not come to discuss the Sunday sermon.

Whenever Molly Gertrude was in need of a spiritual lift she would contact the pastor who would invariably point her back to the Scriptures. But today, there was more on Molly Gertrude's mind than the Good Book. Would Papa Julian be able to shed some light on Charmayne's relationship with Albert Finney, and how much did the man know about Billy's debts?

"Why do you want to know about Charmayne, Albert Finney and Billy?" Papa Julian asked when both Dora and Molly Gertrude were seated in his study, holding a steaming cup of chamomile tea in their hands. He raised his bushy brows and his sharp, but gentle eyes rested on Molly Gertrude. Molly Gertrude didn't mind. She held no secrets from this man.

"Call me crazy...," Molly Gertrude began, her voice trailing off as she was looking for the right words, "... but, what if Abe Mortimer's accident was not an accident at all. To be frank, I am convinced someone was trying to murder him!"

Papa Julian scratched his scalp. "That's quite a statement, Miss Molly Gertrude. What makes you say such a thing?"

"I will tell you, Papa Julian." And thus, Molly Gertrude explained everything she had seen, felt, heard and thought in the last few days. When she was done, Papa Julian pressed his lips together, thought for some time and at last he sighed, "When will we ever learn that we cannot find honey in a pot on which God wrote the words *poison*."

Molly Gertrude arched her brows. "Excuse me?"

The pastor cast her a weary smile. "If people would just stick to the simple rules God has given us, they wouldn't be doing such terrible things to each other."

"Can you tell us something about Albert Finney and Charmayne? Something we don't yet know?" Molly Gertrude asked.

Papa Julian cleared his throat. "Albert Finney was in love with Charmayne. They had plans to get married."

Molly Gertrude's eyes widened. "I never knew that."

"Charmayne and Albert were childhood sweethearts…"

"And…?"

"Then Billy showed up." Papa Julian let out a deep sigh. "Some call him foolish. I call him frivolous. Some call him shady. I call him simple." A sad expression came over his face. "Billy is not a bad kid at heart, but he's really just a big baby and very immature. Abe understood that and he took a fatherly interest in helping him. As a result, Billy came over to the Mortimer's house, joined our church, and swept Charmayne off her feet. The rest is history."

Molly Gertrude's face dropped. "Not good," she mumbled. "Not good at all. And Billy's debts? What do you know about those?"

Papa Julian shrugged his shoulders. "It's a weakness he's working on. He gambles."

Molly Gertrude frowned.

"It's a temptation we've been trying to help him overcome, but I am afraid, not very successfully. He just doesn't seem to be able to fight it. Apparently, he owes a lot of money to somebody."

"But Abe Mortimer has always been good to Billy, right?"

Papa Julian nodded. "I believe Billy was sincere when he handed that first piece of the cake to Abe. Abe was a real father to that boy, and Billy adored him."

"I am just working from the premise that Abe's choking fit was not an accident," Molly Gertrude stated out loud, almost more to herself than to the others in the room. "There was no detectable poison in the cake, at least not as far as we know. However, Billy insisted the first piece of cake was for Abe…

"What if..." Dora interjected with hesitation.

"What?" both Molly Gertrude and Papa Julian asked in unison.

"What if there *was* something wrong with the cake?" Dora explained. "Maybe Albert Finney poisoned that first bite of the cake, hoping to get rid of the competition. But because Billy forced the cake on his father-in-law, it was poor Abe Mortimer who ended up eating it and not Billy."

Molly Gertrude carefully considered Dora's words. At last she shook her head. "I don't know, Dora. It sounds plausible. Still, the lab found no traces of poison in the cake, and if the cake *was* poisoned, do you think Albert would have wanted to run the risk of killing Charmayne in the process?"

Dora shrugged her shoulders. "Stranger things have happened, Miss Molly. Don't they call jealousy the green-eyed monster? Albert Finney's eyes are not only shifty and dark, but I noticed they are green too."

Molly Gertrude pressed her lips together. "Maybe, Dora... Maybe." Then she looked up at Papa Julian and thanked the pastor for his time. "I am sure, pastor, that you prefer a different kind of conversation in your study. We will not take up more of your time, but thank you for your input. You've been a great help."

The pastor blinked his eyes. "It's my pleasure, Miss Molly. What are you going to do now?"

Molly Gertrude smiled. "I will keep following my

hunches, Papa Julian. I am going to take Misty for her afternoon walk, drink coffee in Miss Marmelotte's Tearoom, and..." she turned to Dora, "... I was hoping you could do something for me too."

"Of course," Dora reaffirmed. "What is it?"

"If you could go to the office of the Calmhaven Tribune, and see if you can find anything in their archives about Albert Finney and Billy Monroe's past. No matter how small of an article you may find, it may help us to understand what really happened yesterday."

Dora smiled. The prospect of doing some real detective work seemed appealing to her.

Whatever happened at the wedding, they would uncover the truth. That much was clear.

8

ADVENTURES IN THE TEAROOM

Although Molly Gertrude's pet, Misty, was just a cat, to the old lady she was much more than just a cat. To Molly Gertrude, Misty was like the child she never had, and as a result, not a day went by which Misty did not get spoiled. In fact, some people claimed Molly Gertrude took greater care in feeding Misty than she did herself. In the mornings Misty would get a meal of sardines, meticulously deboned and cooked in milk, and in the evening she would get her share of Molly Gertrude's dinner meat, usually chicken or hamburger.

But that was not all. In the afternoon, Misty would go with Molly Gertrude for her daily stroll to Miss Marmelotte's Tearoom, where, invariably, a saucer filled with whipped cream would be waiting for the purring mouser, prepared by Miss Marmelotte herself. Actually, the charming owner of the tearoom was not a Miss at all, since she had recently married James Buttercup from the Ford garage, but neither she, nor her husband thought it was good business sense to change the name of the tearoom from Miss Marmelotte to Mrs. Marmelotte.

The tearoom was a cozy place, with its interior of wooden paneling, small tables with comfortable seats and a penetrating scent of cake, pie and coffee, and it had been, for a long time, Molly Gertrude and Misty's favorite place every afternoon. And today it was fairly quiet.

In the far left sat a middle aged woman with a blaring, disobedient child, and in the middle two men were involved in a hushed conversation. Hopefully the woman with the screaming brat would soon take control of her situation, for Molly Gertrude did not care for the loud, obstinate howls from the unruly youngster. She wanted to take the time to reflect and normally, there was no better place to do so than Miss Marmelotte's.

"Miss Molly Gertrude Grey and Misty," came the cheerful cry from behind the counter. Mrs. Marmelotte's happy face, framed by her bouncing curls, almost entirely tucked away under her white cap for sanitary reasons, appeared from behind the cash register and shone like the morning sun. Molly Gertrude had grown quite fond of Mrs. Marmelotte, that she suspected had sampled a few too many of her own sugary products. The jolly lady had rightfully earned the adjective *plump* and if she wouldn't take some serious action, the word *fat* would soon follow.

"Sit down," she chirped and pointed to a small table near the far right of the tearoom, which was Molly Gertrude's favorite spot. From there, she could enjoy a good view of the street and bask in the afternoon sun that would warm her stiff, old bones through the window. "Brenda will take your order."

No sooner had she said those words than Brenda, a petite young woman with a brown pony tail, walked up and helped Molly Gertrude into her seat.

"Chamomile tea and raspberry cream pie, I presume?" she mumbled, "... and for Misty, of course, her special Marmelotte's delight, right?"

Molly Gertrude nodded. "Thank you, Brenda."

Minutes later Brenda returned with the ordered goods. Misty's cream, neatly arranged as a twirling pyramid, came on a metal saucer and was placed on the floor right next to Molly Gertrude's feet. Misty began to purr, and after Molly Gertrude had given her cat the green light, the mouser slobbered up the cream with her raspy tongue.

But the disobedient child still kept on screaming.

"I want another cocoa-drink with cream. I don't want milk."

"Why can't I have devil's food cake?"

Molly Gertrude cast the lady with the spoiled kid an angry stare. She came here to think, but how could she concentrate like this?

Spare the rod, spoil the child... but obviously, Molly

Gertrude was not in a position to do any type of work that involved a rod.

An idea formed in her mind.

Maybe the kid would like to see Misty? Didn't the Good Book say to overcome evil with good? That was a better way of restoring the peace than to get all uptight. What was more, Misty, meek as a lamb and almost as old as Methuselah, had shown her ability as a peacemaker before.

Thus, Molly Gertrude pushed her chair away, picked up Misty, and walked with cat in hand to the lady with the screaming child.

Misty did not mind. As long as she was in Molly Gertrude's arms she did not care where they were going, and she softly purred while she nestled herself against Molly Gertrude's chest.

But then, while passing the table with the two men who were still involved in a deep discussion, something startled Molly Gertrude. She overheard something, and she stopped in her tracks.

Did she hear the words Billy Monroe and Abe Mortimer?

She *did*. She was certain.

These two men were talking about the misfortune of Abe Mortimer.

Forgetting about the screaming child near the window on the opposite side, Molly Gertrude stopped near the counter and pretended to read the menu card, all the while pricking up her ears. Hoping not to attract any attention she tried to peer over her shoulder. One of the men seemed strangely familiar, still, she could not place him. She narrowed her eyes and tried to remember if she had ever seen that man before. He was bald, and had dark brown unpleasant eyes. Not the person you would want to meet in a lonely alley on a dark night when you had just missed the last bus home. His black sunglasses were perched on his head, and strangely enough, it almost appeared as if he had no eyebrows.

Surely, someone like would have made an impression, but Molly Gertrude couldn't for the life of her remember when or why he seemed familiar.

The other man was not so, he was stranger in Calmhaven for sure. She turned her glance away from the man and tried to listen more keenly. *If only that child in the corner would start behaving.*

But even though Molly Gertrude could only hear fragments of the conversation, still it was enough to stir her deep interest.

"...Billy is after the inheritance..."

"...Debts..."

"...Family jewels..." *Family jewels? I need to talk to Charmayne about that.*

"...Billy is a killer. He did the old man in..."

Bald-Head stuck up his finger and called out in a dark voice, "Waitress!"

Brenda hurried over to their table.

"Two more coffee liqueur with extra whipped cream," the man ordered without looking at Brenda.

"Coming your way," Brenda responded and she hurried back behind the counter, casting Molly Gertrude a wondering glance as to what the old lady was doing there.

And then, when Brenda returned with the liqueur and the extra cream something went wrong. For the first time in Misty's celebrated life, Molly Gertrude's cat did something very mean. She did something selfish and deeply disturbing. Of course, we are not talking about the great quantity of mice and birds the fat cat had sent over to the next world in her years of earthly service, since those things cannot be considered selfish for a cat. They are only natural. But stealing cream from customers in Marmellotte's Tearoom is not natural, and that's precisely what Misty did.

As soon as the cat saw the luscious layers of cream on top of the coffee liqueur, evenly sprinkled with chocolate flakes, she wormed her way out of Molly Gertrude's arms, and literally flew through the air in order to land on the table of the two men where she began to lap up the cream that was not meant for her.

Molly Gertrude gasped.

So did the two men, and so did Brenda.

And so did the brat in the corner. For the first time since Molly Gertrude had entered the tearoom the kid was silent and stared with big, round eyes at the scene. But it did not take long before more wolfish clamor erupted from his mouth. "Why can't I have a cat like that?"

"Misty…," Molly Gertrude cried out as she rushed to the table of the two men, "…where are your manners." She wanted to run over to tear Misty away from the table. The vibes she had gotten from Bald-Head were bad from the start, and she feared if she were not to interfere immediately Misty would be in serious trouble. But she was too late.

The bald-headed man planted his flat hand against Misty's fur and with a firm swipe of his hand he brushed Misty clear off the table. The cat, complete with cream and chocolate flakes landed on the wooden floor of the tearoom and let out a frustrated *meow*.

Molly Gertrude froze and stared with flashing, dark eyes at Bald-Head. That crook had touched *her* child!

"Stupid cat," the man hissed. He looked up, locked icy eyes with Molly Gertrude and spluttered, "Is that monster yours, lady? You should lock him up in a zoo."

"They should lock you up," Molly Gertrude scoffed. She was so angry she did not care what people thought of her. "Didn't your mother teach you to be kind to animals and speak politely to your elders?"

"Are you the wife of Colonel Blimp or something, old goat?" The man spat out the insult.

"Colonel who?" Molly Gertrude had never heard the expression, but she knew by the tone of Bald-Head's voice, it was meant to be very insulting.

Bald-Head did not answer her question but said with deep, dark hatred, "Your cat is as wicked as the children of Jezebel."

As Molly Gertrude stared deep into the man's eyes, the strange feeling that she had met this man before became only stronger. She had seen him before. But where? Why did he look familiar?

"What are you staring at, old lady?" Bald-Head went on. "Never mind. I am out of here." He turned back to his companion. "This conversation is over."

Mrs. Marmelotte ran over, waving the bill in her hand. "That's twelve dollars."

The man scowled, and actually let out a chuckle that resembled the bloodthirsty laughter of a hyena. "Forget it lady. I am not paying for a monster attack. You won't ever see me again in this place." Without giving Mrs. Marmelotte a chance to respond he got up, turned around and walked out the door. The other man pressed his lips together, pulled out his wallet and dumped a five dollar bill on the table. "My share," he mumbled, and followed his companion.

Everyone was stunned.

Even the spoiled brat in the corner.

"Who was that?" Molly Gertrude asked at last when both men had left the scene.

Mrs. Marmelotte shrugged her shoulders. "Never saw him before. He's a shady one if you ask me."

All at once, it came to Molly Gertrude what she was to do next. But she had to act quickly.

"Do you mind if Misty stays here a bit longer?" she asked the owner of the tearoom, while waving both index fingers nervously before Mrs. Marmelotte in the air.

Mrs. Marmelotte stared at her, not quite understanding the question. "Sure... but why?"

"I'll be back," Molly Gertrude said, "but I've got somewhere to go." As soon as she had received the assurance Misty was in good hands, she grabbed her coat and walking cane, and hurried to the door. She had no idea why, but she had the distinct feeling she had to find out more about this strange bald-headed man who had been so rude to Misty.

9

MORE PUZZLE PIECES FALL
INTO PLACE

The sun was already going down when the taxi stopped in front of Molly Gertrude's house, and Molly Gertrude, clutching Misty under her arm, climbed out with much sighing and mumbling.

The taxi driver, a young fellow with fat, thick lips and unwashed, greasy hair, did not seem the least bit interested in helping an old lady out of his cab, and refused to get out of his seat in order to assist. He just wanted the money, a good tip, and to be off to greener pastures. But as far as Molly Gertrude was concerned, he would have to find these pastures without her tip. She had seen more than enough rude, shifty people for one day, and, although she was normally a very generous and gracious person, right now she felt like a regular battle-ax. After she paid the boy the exact amount of dollars it stated on his taxi meter, she shook her head and without saying another word she turned and walked to her porch.

"Miss Molly... I've been waiting here for over an hour?" A concerned voice from off the porch washed over her.

"Dora? What are you doing here?" Molly Gertrude was ever so glad to see the familiar, trustworthy face of dear Dora, but she had not expected it.

Dora's answer got lost in the noise the taxi driver made with his cab. The man, irritated he had not gotten his tip, decided to do the best he could to reveal the obstinate state of his heart and roared off in a huff with screeching tires, producing a cloud of dust, dirt and gravel.

"What was that?" Dora wondered while she arched her brows.

Molly Gertrude climbed up the stairs and shrugged her shoulders. "I don't know what this world is coming to, Dora. People like that young man in the taxi will be the rulers of tomorrow."

Dora bit her lower lip. "Rough day, huh?"

Molly Gertrude nodded. "Tell me about it." She fished her house keys out of her coat pocket and opened the door. "But why are you here, Dora? Have you been waiting a long time?"

Dora nodded. "For about an hour. I was getting worried about you, Miss Molly. You are never gone by yourself for that long. If you had a smartphone you could have called me, and I would have driven you around."

Molly Gertrude gave Dora a pained stare. "No

smartphone, Dora. You know the rules." As she stuck the key into the lock she added, "Did you find out something? Is that why you are here?"

A secretive smile appeared on Dora's face. "Yes, that's why I am here Miss Molly. I found out something about Billy's past..." She lowered her voice as if she were afraid the butterflies could not be trusted. "We'll talk inside."

Molly Gertrude looked up, surprise etched on her face. "I found out things too, Dora. Let's talk, but no cookies today. Just tea."

As soon as Dora entered the house she began to talk about her findings.

"It was difficult at first. They have this really old database for the Calmhaven Tribune. They only began to digitalize their archives about 10 years ago. Everything from before is on dusty, old filmstrips, and it took me a full hour to understand how the whole thing even worked. But once I got the hang of it I was fascinated to read about happenings from over 15 years ago."

Molly Gertrude nodded. "Those were the days. And... what did you find?"

"Nothing," Dora stated firmly. "I realized I was barking up the wrong tree."

"How's that?"

"Billy Monroe is a young man. He just turned 25. Ten years ago he was 15, which means that even if he had done something fishy, his name wouldn't be mentioned in the papers. I was wasting my time, searching through those musty, old files. I could just use their digital database. All I had to do was start a string of searches on Billy Monroe and Albert Finney, and the database spewed out lots of stuff." Dora smacked her lips.

"Lots of stuff?" Molly Gertrude narrowed her eyes.

"Most of it can be ruled out." Dora made a sign with her hand as if she was wiping the stuff away. 'You know stuff about Albert Finney winning a cake competition in Alberta, and Billy Monroe getting a third-place medal in Calmhaven's ping-pong tournament, but...," she waited, presumably to heighten the tension, "... there was one rather obscure little article from nine years ago."

"Oh?"

"I made a copy of it, so you could read it for yourself." Dora pulled a printed note from her bag and handed it to Molly Gertrude, who unfolded it.

JUVENILE CRIME ON THE RISE IN CALMHAVEN:
DUSTIN MOOLWORTH. CALMHAVEN

25 March 2009

Despite the heroic efforts of Pastor Julian and the Calmhaven Trinity Church, crime stops for no one. And as we all know, crime often starts young as it seems to have an uncanny, almost magnetic pull on young people. B. Monroe is its latest victim. The 16-year-old, together with a youngster whose name cannot be revealed due to his age, was caught breaking into the house of Abraham Melvin Mortimer, where they caused destruction of property and were ultimately caught two hours later in a local youth club in Calmhaven.

B. Monroe, son of J.D. Monroe, who is still serving a five-year prison sentence in Auburn, and his mother, Clara Monroe-Baines, who left Calmhaven a year ago without leaving a forwarding address, has up till this moment been taken care of by Pastor Julian and the elders of the church, but clearly, even the influence of our beloved minister seems to have its limitations. All stolen items have been returned to Abraham Mortimer except for a rare piece of jewelry, an heirloom that belonged to Abraham's late wife who passed away ten years ago in a tragic boat accident. Both boys declared not to know anything about jewelry. But who believes the word of a thief?

Judge Arrow will decide the case on a yet to be determined date.

"What do you think of that?" Dora whispered. "Bill Monroe actually broke into Abe's house and has managed to marry the man's daughter. He insists on the man eating the cake first, and seconds later poor Abe is on the floor…"

Molly Gertrude nodded while thinking it over. At last she licked her lips and said, "Sometimes the crime is obvious, but more often than not, when it's so obvious, it is likely to be a red herring. What's more, we haven't an iota of proof that there was something wrong with that cake. It's only guess work."

"I know," Dora sighed. "But what's your gut feeling about this?"

"As I said," Molly Gertrude shrugged, "I am not sure. Papa Julian lived with Billy for quite some time, and he actually thinks Billy is not such a bad boy, but simply lacks guidance and direction."

A small scowl appeared on Dora's face. "Of course Papa Julian says that. That man loves everyone and if need be, he will even see the good in a cockroach."

Molly Gertrude raised her brows. "That's quite a statement. You could also consider the man has a bit of wisdom and discernment."

Dora blushed. "Sorry, Miss Molly… I know I shouldn't say such things. It's just when you discover bits and pieces of the puzzle your mind sometimes runs ahead of you."

Molly Gertrude gave her a smile. "It's no problem, Dora. I know the feeling, and to ease your heart, I haven't ruled out Billy at all. I just don't want to jump to conclusions that will only serve to cloud my mind and make it harder to see the more hidden signs." She smacked with her lips, and then asked, "No more? Nothing about Judge Arrow?"

Dora shook her head. "Nothing else. And you? What were you doing in that taxi?"

Molly Gertrude sighed. "I was doing some good old-fashioned snooping around.

Dora's eyes widened. "Where?"

"You ever been to Waterside Snomp?"

"Not very often," Dora admitted. "Calmhaven is but a small town, but even we have our poor area."

"Yes we do," Molly Gertrude agreed. "I went there today. I followed a man there."

"A man? Who?"

Molly Gertrude pressed her lips together. "I do not know his name, but he was in Miss Marmelotte's Tearoom with a buddy of his…"

"And…?"

"I overheard them discussing Abe Mortimer and Billy's debts." As Molly Gertrude relived the event, new anger rose as she recalled how the wretched man had swatted Misty away as if she were a mere flea.

Dora's eyes widened as she noticed Molly Gertrude's anger rising. "W-What happened?'

"All I know is the man is shady, he hates cats almost as much as he hates life and…," she hesitated, "… I have seen him before somewhere, but I don't know where."

"What did he look like?" Dora's mind was working overtime again.

As Molly Gertrude gave the description, Dora looked puzzled. "Doesn't ring a bell."

"Anyway," Molly Gertrude continued, "I left Misty at the tearoom and followed the man as best as I could. It took me a great deal of strength, but luckily Calmhaven is not yet as big as New York, and soon I saw he was going to Waterside Snomp." Molly Gertrude shook her head. "He's staying in a house, a shack really, at the edge of town."

"And you really don't know where you know this man from?"

Molly Gertrude shook her head. "But he's unusual. When I first looked into his eyes I had this strange tingling, burning sensation again in my left shoulder."

"And?"

"I told you. I get that sometimes when I am face to face with an important clue. Call it whatever you want. Old ladies intuition. All I know is that the feeling only shows up when there's something I need to know."

Dora rearranged her glasses. "So, what now?"

"We break in."

Dora's face became white. "We do *what*?"

"We break in," Molly Gertrude repeated in a calm voice, as if she were discussing whether or not to buy cheese in the Cash'em-Right or in the MacGover's, where things were generally a bit more expensive.

"We can't do that, Miss Molly."

"Of course we can," Molly Gertrude already had it all figured out. "I noticed his garage door is not locked. The wood seems rotten and apparently, the fellow doesn't even care."

"But how do you know he won't be home?"

Molly Gertrude shrugged. "We don't. But if my feelings are right, a man like that will not be sitting in his lonely shack at night. He'll be drinking it up in the bar with his buddies. And, if perchance he is home… well, then we will have to wait."

"But, breaking in is illegal… and, eh…" she hesitated, "… it's dangerous."

"But… it's exciting as well." Molly Gertrude leaned forward and narrowed her eyes as she stared at Dora. "We're not stealing, or robbing from the poor… We are only figuring out what happened to poor Abe Mortimer. And, did you know…", she arched her brows, "That this man hit Misty…"

Anger flashed over Dora's face. "He did?"

"He sure did," Molly Gertrude replied as she picked up Misty from the floor and placed the cat on her lap. "He's a brute, and no doubt as wicked as the children of Jezebel." Molly Gertrude chuckled, "Those were his own words when he talked about Misty."

Molly Gertrude couldn't help but smile when she saw

Dora's facial muscles tighten and she heard her assistant say with determination, "When do we break in?" The disgust was almost dripping from her face.

"Tomorrow evening," Molly Gertrude replied. "But in the morning I want you to call Deputy Digby."

"Oh? What for?" Dora blushed.

"Maybe he can find out for us what happened with Billy after he was caught stealing. I would also be interested in knowing who Billy's buddy in crime was."

Dora nodded and let out a satisfied little sigh. "We made good progress today, Miss Molly."

"I believe we did, Dora. Every day it seems we're getting a tiny step closer to solving the puzzle."

SHERIFF BARNES

"Hello, you are talking to Calmhaven's Police Station. Belinda Sommersby speaking. How may I help you?" Dora hesitated. She had hoped to immediately get Deputy Digby on the line, but of course that was wishful thinking. Belinda Sommersby was the one who received almost all of the calls to the office.

"How may I help you?" Belinda's melodious voice repeated her question.

"Hello, you are speaking with Dora Brightside. I was hoping to talk to Deputy Digby, please."

"He's on patrol, Ma'am. May I leave a message?"

On patrol? "No, Miss Sommersby. I can try later."

"Wait," came the voice on the other side. "I'll give you

Sheriff Barnes. After all, he's the one with all the knowledge, anyway. We aim to please, Ma'am."

"No... eh...," Dora protested, but it appeared Belinda Sommersby had left her post and was informing Sheriff Barnes somebody wanted to talk to the police.

This was not the way she wanted things to go. Deputy Digby would listen to her, but JJ Barnes would certainly not be willing to give her any information regarding Billy Monroe's antics about ten years ago. What was she going to tell the man?

Not even half a minute later Barnes' dark voice echoed through the receiver. "Sheriff Barnes speaking. Who am I talking to?"

"Hello, Mr. Barnes," Dora piped trying to sound enthusiastic. "This is Dora Brightside. I-I was wondering if you have... erm... any news."

It was silent for a few moments. Then Barnes barked. "What news?"

"You know... about the unfortunate circumstances surrounding Abe Mortimer?" Dora had no idea what else to say.

"Why do you ask?" Barnes queried. Then he answered his own question. "Miss Grey asked you to call, right? You are the assistant of Miss Grey's Cozy Bridal Agency."

"That's right, Sir," Dora echoed. Dora expected irritation,

but instead, and to her relief, JJ Barnes let out a chuckle. "You two ladies are not giving up easily, are you?"

"No, Sir," Dora acknowledged.

"Well, there's nothing to add that Miss Grey doesn't already know," Sheriff Barnes added. "There's still nothing whatever that gives us any reason to think poor Abe Mortimer was being targeted by a ruthless murderer. No new information came up."

"Nothing at all?"

"No, Miss Brightside, nothing at all. Just meaningless stuff we found in the pocket of his pants."

Dora pricked up her ears. "What did you find?"

"The usual stuff," JJ Barnes replied with another chuckle. Dora felt the man was not taking her seriously. He was humoring her, thinking that neither she nor Molly Gertrude were capable of doing proper detective work. She decided to run the risk of irritating or even offending the man.

"What's the usual stuff, Sheriff?"

Barnes sighed. "Come on, Miss Brightside. Simple stuff. A hanky, a receipt from the Cash'em-Right, confetti from the wedding and a wrinkled business card from a dentist in another town."

Dora clucked her tongue. "Doesn't seem very important."

"My point, Miss Brightside. And if you want to excuse me

now, I've got some real work to do." He was annoyed. He was just about to hang up the phone when he remembered something. "Oh... by the way..."

"Yes?"

"Could you ask Miss Grey to give me a call? There's something I wish to discuss with her."

Dora tilted her head. "I-Is she in trouble?"

"No, Miss Brightside. She's not." JJ Barnes actually laughed. "Just ask her to call. That's all. Bye, bye." Without waiting for Dora's reply, he hung up the phone.

Dora sighed. At least she had not totally angered the Sheriff. But getting the information that Molly Gertrude had asked her for would not be easy. There was no way she was going to call the police station again.

But she did not have to.

Only half an hour after Sheriff Barnes had hung up, Dora's mobile phone rang.

When Dora glanced at the screen, her heart took a small leap. It said the caller was Digby.

She pushed the *accept call* button and cried out, "Digby... you called." Realizing she sounded weird to someone who had no foreknowledge of what had transpired, she tried to temper her enthusiasm and switched to a reserved business tone. "Dora Brightside speaking. How may I help you?"

On the other side, Digby was probably scratching his head, but at last the man spoke. "Miss Brightside? I was so happy you called, and now I am just returning your call."

"Thank you Digby," Dora answered feeling rather lame. "I-eh… well I was just wondering about something…"

"Sure," Digby responded. "May I call you, Dora? It… it doesn't sound so formal. All that Digby and Miss Brightside stuff. The Calmhaven police are here to serve you, but I work better on a first name basis. Actually…," he hesitated, "before we talk about your business, I was wondering about something myself as well."

"Oh?" Dora walked over to her couch and sank down.

"Yeah erm…," Digby mumbled. He sounded nervous, and he did not finish. His sentence kept hanging in the air.

"What is it, Digby?" Dora asked, thinking whatever was on Digby's mind would be best solved before she troubled him with her request about Billy Monroe and his young buddy in crime.

"What is on your mind?" Dora prompted. She could clearly hear Digby licking his lips over the phone.

"Well… you know, I've been on the force now for quite a number of years…"

"Congratulations!"

"It's been a mile stone experience, serving the Calmhaven police force," he continued.

"I can imagine," Dora mumbled. "And?"

"Well... eh, I am hoping to learn a lot in the years to come..." Dora narrowed her eyes. What was Digby trying to say?

"You know JJ is getting on in years. This week he's turning 55, and if I continue to make progress, as I am doing right now, he'll make me the new Sheriff..." His voice now had an urgent ring to it. "You understand what I am saying, Dora?" Digby stopped as he was preparing for a high jump and then, all at once, he mumbled while almost stumbling over his words, "I may very well be Calmhaven's future Sheriff..."

"That would be wonderful, Digby, truly," Dora managed to say. "But why are you telling me this?"

Digby cleared his throat. "I'll come straight to the point, Dora. I... eh..."

Dora listened, but no point came.

At last his voice appeared over the phone again. "I like you, Miss Dora... And, even though I am not yet Calmhaven's Sheriff, I'd like to..."

Dora blushed. She was glad this was not a Skype call as then Digby would have seen it.

"W-What do you mean?"

"I would like to get to know you better," he continued. "Next Saturday, Sheriff JJ is having his 55th birthday, and he is organizing a dance... Would you be my partner?"

"I-I…" Dora stammered, "…can't dance."

"Neither can I," Digby replied. "But I wouldn't want to be going there with anybody else. Would you like to come? No strings attached. Just an evening at JJ's holiday house."

Dora did not know what to say. She did like Digby, but it probably wouldn't work out very well. It never did for her. Even her so-called *best* friend, when she was still at school, had told her once in a moment of anger that she was the ugly duckling of Calmhaven and therefore destined to stay single. "C-Can I think about it?" she finally managed to say. That was a good answer as it felt safe, and it left all the options open.

"Sure," came Digby's reply. He sounded disappointed. "And… eh, why did you call me?"

"Call you?" Dora had completely forgotten about the reason she had contacted Digby in the first place. "Of course." She let out a nervous chuckle and then explained what Molly Gertrude had asked of her. "Nine years ago Billy Monroe was caught breaking in Abe Mortimer's house. He and a young lad were arrested. Would you be able to check the records and let me know what happened? Did Billy get punished, and who was the other boy?"

Digby sighed. "More secret stuff for Miss Grey, I presume?"

"A little," Dora croaked. "Will you do it?"

"Sure," Digby replied, "if you promise to think about going with me to JJ's party."

"That's a promise, Digby."

"Good," Digby said. "I'll call you as soon as I know more."

11

THE BREAK-IN

Molly Gertrude and Dora, in preparation for the break-in at the house of Bald-Head, had clothed themselves like regular spies. Both women wore a long, dark overcoat and a hat, and Dora had even exchanged her regular glasses for her sunglasses. Molly Gertrude had suggested that wasn't necessary, and it would even hinder her driving, but Dora insisted on being as inconspicuous as she could, and at last Molly Gertrude consented.

That afternoon Dora had told Molly Gertrude all about her conversations with both JJ Barnes and Dawson Digby, and had mentioned as well that the Sheriff wanted to talk to Molly.

"Talk to me? Why?"

"I don't know," Dora wondered. "He said, you weren't in trouble."

"Of course I am not in trouble," Molly Gertrude grunted. "I am too old for that. Well, he can wait until tomorrow. First we have a break-in to perform."

Dora had not wanted to talk about Digby's invitation to accompany him to Barnes' birthday dance. Molly Gertrude was way too old to dance anyway and it seemed useless information for her elderly friend.

As they stepped out of the house and headed towards Dora's Kia Rio the sun was just sinking behind the distant mountains. It wouldn't be long before it was dark.

"All right," Dora said, as both women were seated. "Where to now?"

"You know," Molly Gertrude stated. "Waterside Snomp."

"And once we have arrived?"

"There's a small Cash-'em-Right there. We'll pull up in the parking lot and from there we can just see the house. Soon, it will be dark, so if that wretched fellow is home there will be lights on, and we'll have to wait."

As Dora revved up the engine she bit her lower lip. "What are we actually hoping to find in his house?"

"I don't know," Molly Gertrude replied. "Maybe we'll find nothing. But I have this strange conviction there's more to this man than we know at the moment." As they took off she began to guide Dora to Waterside Snomp.

About ten minutes later they arrived at the parking lot of

a small Cash-'em-Right and Dora parked in such a way that they had a good view of the house.

Molly Gertrude had not said too much. Waterside Snomp was run-down, and the house in question was no exception. Squeezed in between two bulkier buildings, the house they wanted to break into seemed a bit crooked, almost as if it were trying to escape the grip of the other two buildings. It was a two-story house, with a porch that looked rather unsteady, and all of the wood was in desperate need of a paint job. The windows were covered with an odd assortment of curtains, which did not match.

"That's it?" Dora cringed.

Molly Gertrude nodded without answering. In front of the house was a tiny garden not even half as big as Molly Gertrude's kitchen. It was overgrown with weeds and nettles, but Bald-Head had carved out a path to the porch.

"When we go in...," Molly Gertrude whispered, even though there was nobody else around, "... we go down to the garage. That door is open."

"You've already been there, huh?" Dora clucked her tongue. Molly Gertrude did not cease to amaze her.

Molly Gertrude did not answer but kept peering at the house some fifty feet away from where they were sitting.

"You reckon anybody is home?" Dora asked.

"There's no light," Molly Gertrude answered. "We wait just

a wee bit longer. When the darkness has fully set in we will know for sure."

And so the two wedding planners kept staring at the hideout of Bald-Head until darkness had fully covered the town.

There was still no light in the house.

Molly Gertrude said. "We're going in."

Minutes later both women stood before the rusty fence of the house they wanted to investigate. All the curtains were halfway open. There was no mistake possible. Nobody was home. As Molly Gertrude opened the little gate, it made a terrifying creak. Dora froze, but Molly Gertrude just shrugged her shoulders. "It's nothing, Dora. The guy needs to learn to take care of his property. What a mess it is here."

"It's hard to see anything," Dora complained.

"Of course, it is," Molly Gertrude snorted. "I told you not to bring your sun glasses."

Dora blushed and took them off. However, she had not thought of taking her regular glasses along and thus her sight was greatly limited. "C-Can I hold your hand, Miss Molly" she pleaded. "I am afraid I am going to sprain my ankle."

Molly Gertrude shook her head. "That's not going to

work," she said as she plucked a camping flashlight out of her long overcoat. "Maybe it's best if you stay as the lookout, here in the garden. If anything happens, or if Bald-Head comes back, you can then warn me."

"How do I do that? I can't see a thing."

"You don't only need eyes to be a good detective," Molly Gertrude replied in a determined voice. "Use your ears." It was clear this was the way Molly Gertrude wanted it, as the old lady turned around and while leaning on her cane, she descended the three stony steps that led to the garage door.

She had been right in her assessment about the door being unlocked. As she stood before it, she gave the moldy wood a gentle push with her walking cane. It swung open with another creak. This one not nearly as loud as the one the metal fence had produced. A dark hole opened before her, and a musty smell of unwashed clothes and mold entered her nostrils.

Great. This is going to be a fun excursion. Molly Gertrude clicked on her flashlight. It produced a firm ray of light that illuminated a bunch of car tires that were haphazardly tossed on the ground before her, and reflected off a mirror that stood against the wall on the opposite side. Molly Gertrude narrowed her eyes as she scanned the area with bated breath.

"What do you see?" Dora cried out in a hoarse whisper from behind.

"Sssht," Molly Gertrude fired back. "We don't need any unnecessary attention."

Molly Gertrude directed the flashlight in all corners of the garage. Just mess. Lots of mess, but nothing that would give any clue as to Bald-Head's involvement in Abe Mortimer's misfortune.

Just as she spotted the door to the upstairs, she was alerted by a loud ring coming from the front yard.

Dora's mobile phone. It was loud and clear. She should have turned it off. Molly Gertrude was strengthened again in her conviction that mobile phones were not a blessing.

Molly Gertrude hurried back, trying to tell Dora to turn it off, but the girl had already taken the call and was talking over the phone in a hushed voice.

"Turn it off," Molly Gertrude hissed to Dora from the bottom of the three steps.

"I can't," Dora whispered back. "It's Digby."

Digby? Why on God's good earth is that man calling while they were breaking into the house of a serious murder suspect?

"Thank you, Digby," she heard Dora's clear voice rumbling through the quiet of the night. "I'll tell Miss Molly. And my answer to you? It's a yes."

What was she talking about? Oh Lord, help Dora to hang up! To Molly Gertrude's great relief her prayer was answered almost instantly, as she heard Dora say, "Bye then. See you on Saturday."

It was quiet again.

"Psst, Dora...?"

"What?"

"Please turn that thing off."

"Sure."

"Stay on the alert, okay? I am going back in." Without waiting for a reply Molly Gertrude turned and headed back to the door that hopefully would lead her into the main house.

Dora scolded herself. How could she have been so dumb as to forget her proper glasses. Now, for the first time ever, she was part of something so exciting, something so out of the ordinary that such things only happened in books. But at the crucial moment she couldn't do a thing. She glared at her sunglasses as if they were her worst nightmare and grunted. At least Digby had called. That was nice.

Of course, Molly Gertrude had gotten quite upset, and rightfully so, but at least Digby had brought good news. Digby had been doing some snooping around in the archives and had found out what had happened to Billy and his unnamed crony after their arrest. Abe Mortimer had not wanted to press charges. The gentleman had made some kind of deal with Billy that if the youngster would get a lot more serious about religion in his life, this theft could be forgiven. Billy, of course, had been more than happy to comply. He would have done just about anything in order to stay out of the clutches of the law.

It appeared, however, the missing jewelry was never recovered.

Dora tried to picture how Digby had been going through the archives, knowing that JJ Barnes would not be pleased if he found out his deputy was doing some research for Molly Gertrude Grey. She could see him going through the archives with his focused, bright eyes, a lock of his blond hair coming out from under his police cap, and his tongue slightly sticking out of his mouth as he concentrated to the full to find the information they had asked for.

Dora wondered if Digby liked going by his last name. She rather liked the sound of Dawson, but everyone was so used to calling the young deputy, Digby, it would seem almost strange to call him anything else. She wouldn't be too keen if people would constantly call her Brightside. *Brightside bring the mail. You want coffee, Brightside? Turn off your mobile phone, Brightside.* It gave the idea she was in some sort of army, which was the last place she ever wanted to be. Either way, Digby or Dawson, she had agreed to go with him to JJ Barnes' party. That made her feel good. Even Molly Gertrude had hinted to the fact that maybe, just maybe, there was a chance of something—

Dora heard something.

A few people were coming down the street in their direction. They were probably still near the Cash'em-Right… still far, but they were definitely heading this way. Even though it was still early, they had clearly been drinking, as their voices were too loud, too overbearing and lacked any sense of decency.

"Miss Molly… careful, somebody's coming this way," Dora whispered, but of course, Molly Gertrude would not hear such utterances in a thousand years. Just then Dora saw the light of Molly Gertrude's flashlight going through the upstairs room. She should have closed the curtains.

Dora put on her sunglasses and sprinted to the entrance and swung her head around the iron gate in order to see if people were indeed coming their way. She couldn't see clearly as there were no street lamps in this part of town, but judging by the noise and the footsteps that were rapidly coming closer they would be passing the place soon.

"Oh, dear Lord in Heaven," Dora prayed as she ran back. She jerked her sunglasses off again as they made it impossible to see anything without light. She had to warn Molly Gertrude to turn off that stupid flashlight.

The voices were now right near the gate.

"Hey J-Jack…Another one? I still have a bah-bah-b-bottle-eh… in the ga-garage."

While somebody pushed and rattled the iron gate, another raw voice burst out in a howling scream, confirming another taste from the bah-bah-bottle in the garage would be his delight.

Dora's heart froze. They were not just pedestrians passing by, they were heading to this very house. She looked up as drops of sweat formed on her forehead. The light of the flashlight was still clearly visible in the upper room. The rays were poking around as Molly Gertrude shone it in every corner. *Turn it off, Molly... For Heaven's sake.*

But Dora had no more time to do anything else. The intruders were almost upon her. A bitter taste entered Dora's mouth as she realized that no matter how wicked these people may be, she and Molly Gertrude were the true intruders. Hoping not to stumble and fall she jumped the three steps down towards the garage door and heaved a sigh of relief when she landed without spraining her ankle on the stones. Immediately she crouched down behind a garbage container right outside the garage door. That's when she noticed the garage door was still half open. Too late. There was nothing she could do.

She could not clearly see but saw the vague silhouettes of three man climbing up onto the porch. A smell of liquor and smoke hung around them and it made Dora cringe.

"C-Can't f-find the keyhole," one of them slurred.

"Gimme that key," another one hollered. He had a strange croak to his voice and Dora decided that if frogs could talk, that's what they would sound like.

Somehow Frogman managed to get the door open and the three drunks stumbled inside. A second later they slammed the door closed. She was safe... but Molly Gertrude? Poor Miss Molly. She was still in the house.

1 2
CONFRONTATIONS

Dora felt utterly defeated as she stumbled back to the parking lot of the Cash'em-Right. Seeing her faithful Kia Rio cheered her heart somewhat. The metal of the chassis shone joyfully in welcome to its mistress as the light of the supermarket reflected on the second-hand car.

But Dora's heart did not shine.

Molly Gertrude was in serious danger, and as Dora had run back to the car, she had already envisioned a few of the most horrible scenario's. *Molly Gertrude half dead in the hospital. Or worse, Molly Gertrude completely dead in an alley. Still worse, Molly Gertrude gone, never to be heard of again.*

Dora was well aware of Mark Twain's famous statement he made in his latter days in which he proclaimed that he was an old man who had seen many troubles in his life. But he was quick to add, *'Most of them never happened.'* But tonight she was sure Twain was wrong, as something very bad was about to happen to dear Miss Molly. What could Molly Gertrude do to defend herself against these thugs if they found out she had broken into their house? It even made it worse that these were not normal thugs, but intoxicated thugs. People with alcohol streaming through their veins were unpredictable and could make the weirdest decisions.

"Dear Lord," she lifted up her eyes to the roof of the car, "...what am I to do?'

But instead of a booming answer from the heavens, her interior light began to waver. Dora tapped it with her finger, causing it to stop working altogether.

Great.

Should she call Digby? That was possibly her best option. JJ Barnes was a foghorn, and although the man did have more authority, she really didn't like the idea of calling the Sheriff. No, calling Digby was her best option.

She plucked her mobile phone out of her coat pocket, and wanted to push the call-button. But as she stared at the screen, she realized she could not even read the numbers on the dial. She needed her sunglasses again. Luckily the screen lit up, and with her sunglasses perched on her nose, she could finally call in the cavalry.

With trembling fingers she tapped Digby's number. He did not pick up right away. Maybe he was busy... She waited with bated breath as the phone kept on trying to make the connection. At last, and to Dora's great relief, Digby picked up.

"Dora," he jubilantly yelled, as he had apparently recognized the number. "What can I do for you?"

"Digby... It's Miss Molly," Dora began. She wanted to say more, but right at that instant, somebody was knocking loud and insistent on the window, effectively interrupting her talk. *Oh, Lord, please don't let me have too many of these nights.* She turned her head, and let out a yelp. There stood Molly Gertrude, unharmed, healthy, and looking very prim. "Can you let me in," she called, her voice barely audible through the closed window. "And who are you calling?"

"Dora? Hello... what's going on?" Digby's voice rang through the car as Dora, in her excitement, had pushed the speakerphone button by mistake.

"I-I..." Dora shouted in her phone, "... don't know."

"Let me in," Molly Gertrude called from the outside. She was getting impatient. "We need to get out of here." That was the understatement of the year.

Dora yanked the door to the passenger seat open and helped Molly Gertrude in.

"Is Miss Grey there?" Digby's voice came again through the loudspeaker. "Miss Grey? Is that you?"

Dora wanted to answer him but Molly Gertrude was first. Since the speakerphone was on, she knew Digby could hear her words even though she was not speaking directly into the phone. "Go home, Digby. You need your rest. I'll take it from here."

"But I *am* home," Digby protested. "What's going on?"

"Bye Digby," Molly Gertrude ordered in a stiff voice. "Thank you for your good work. See you soon." She turned her eyes to Dora and even though not a word was spoken, Dora could clearly hear Miss Molly's voice in her heart: "Turn-It-Off!"

"Bye Digby," she still managed to say. "See you soon." Then she turned off the phone, and as she fell back in her seat she let out a long, tired sigh. After she had closed her eyes for a second, she turned her glance at Miss Molly and said, "I will never do this again. Not ever…"

Molly Gertrude arched her brows. "Not so negative, dear Dora. It was a most profitable evening. I am sure glad we went."

Dora stared with disbelieving eyes at Miss Molly. "You almost got caught by some local drunks. Do you know what they could have done to you? Such fellows do not believe in God nor man. You were in serious danger."

"No, I wasn't," Molly Gertrude snorted. "These fellows were so drunk I heard them coming from a mile away. I made my way back to the garage in time. But tell me," she exclaimed. "Why did you call Digby?"

Dora's face dropped and she suppressed a sob. "I was

scared for you, Miss Molly. Really scared. I did not know what to do, so I thought I'd call Digby."

Molly Gertrude seemed surprised, but then a tender expression washed over her face, and she grabbed Dora's hand. "Thank you, dear Dora, for being my assistant. I am an old lady, and I suppose I am not as much aware of the dangers anymore as you are. But I appreciate your friendship more than you know. I am sorry to have scared you."

Dora's eyes glistened for a moment, but then she forced a smile on her face. "Tell me... what did you find?"

Molly Gertrude tilted her head. "I don't know if it has much meaning, but this man, Bald-Head, isn't always bald."

Dora's eyes widened. "He isn't?"

"I found three wigs, and a stash of what looked like moustaches – I'm not certain. They were more like hairy caterpillars. Yeuck!"

Dora narrowed her eyes. "Why would anyone have three wigs and, em, hairy caterpillars?"

"It's simple," Molly Gertrude said. "You only have three wigs if you want to disguise yourself. Of course, it's still too early to tell if Bald-Head is connected to Abe Mortimer's unfortunate encounter with a killer cake, but I am convinced he's a slippery character. That much is certain."

"Anything else?"

"He works different jobs. I found all sorts of outfits stuffed into his overcrowded wardrobe."

Dora shrugged her shoulder. "That's normal. Any man has to work for a living."

"Of course," Molly Gertrude repeated while she nodded her head. "But some men make an honest living, while there are others who prefer to make a dishonest living. I have the feeling that our friend Bald-Head falls in the second category."

"Can we go now?" Dora asked while she shivered.

Molly Gertrude smiled. "We can, Dora." Her eyes lit up as she thought of something. "If you come in for a cup of tea I have a surprise for you."

"What?"

"I baked a homemade batch."

"Of what?"

Molly Gertrude frowned. "Come on Dora, you know. I made them this afternoon, especially for you."

"Silky Citrus Curd Cookies?"

Molly Gertrude nodded. "There's no better remedy for ruffled nerves. Let's go."

∽

Billy's face paled as he stared at Charmayne. "You can't be serious, honey. You actually went to see Molly Gertrude Grey and asked her to investigate your father's incident at the wedding? Look, I know your Daddy is still in a coma, but everyone knows it was an accident. He choked on the cake. I'm certain he will be ok," he said, almost choking himself on the final words. Charmayne took it as an indication that he too was upset by the whole affair, but just did not know how to quite express himself.

She shook her head. "It was no accident, Billy."

Billy thought it over. "But who would do such a thing?" A dark cloud washed over his face and his eyes grew wide. "You don't think I have anything to do with it, do you, Charmayne?" His breath came in short gasps as he began to realize that if Abe Mortimer breathed his last, he would be one of the first suspects.

Charmayne looked up at her husband. "Billy, we are just starting out on the road together. It's not going to be an easy ride, but let me make one thing clear…"

Billy took a step back. "Sure… eh, what's that?"

"I should have had this conversation much earlier. But this whole affair has made one thing very, very clear…"

Billy tilted his head. He wasn't certain if he liked what was coming.

"For our marriage to even have a chance of success we need to really work on our relationship."

"Sure, anything you say."

"I want you to be honest with me. Completely honest."

"Of course, Charmayne. I am always honest."

"Are you, Billy?" She rested her eyes on Billy. Billy began to fumble with the button on the cuff of his shirt and his eyes began to dart. "I had nothing to do with what happened to your Pop, Charmayne. You must believe me. I loved him like the father I never had."

"I believe you, Billy," Charmayne said, "but there are other issues."

"Other issues? What do you mean?"

I heard you have debts. Big debts."

Billy's cheeks flushed red and his mouth opened and closed as if he were a fish on dry land. "How do you…? I mean, sure, I have a few debts, but it's nothing I can't handle."

"But this is the first time you are admitting those debts to me personally. A few days *after* we have gotten married."

Billy threw up his arms in the air. "Please, Charmayne, it's a storm in a glass of water. Who told you I've got debts? I bet it's your old boyfriend, Albert Finney. Are you still seeing him?" Billy gritted his teeth. "You are talking about honesty, but at the same time you still see Albert behind my back."

A pained expression washed over Charmayne's face.

"That's not fair, Billy. I married you, didn't I? And it wasn't Albert who told me."

Billy's eyes widened. "It wasn't?"

"No Billy, it was my Daddy. Charmayne gently slapped with her hand on the couch and with her eyes she demanded that Billy sit down next to her. Billy almost looked like a little schoolboy as he came near and sat down. "Listen, Billy… from now on, it's honesty. You tell me everything, and I will tell you everything too. I have always known about your gambling problems, but I've also always wanted to give you a chance, just like my Daddy. But now that we are married, it's time to be completely open and start changing."

Billy was still gasping for air. "I-I am sorry Charmayne. I will change. Honestly."

"If you are going to be honest with me it will work, Billy."

Billy scratched his forehead. "It's not exactly fair."

"It isn't? Why not?"

"You don't have any secrets," Billy objected.

"Yes, I do," Charmayne answered.

Billy stared at her, not understanding what she meant.

"Shall I tell you one of my secrets, Billy?"

"Please…"

"My Daddy took your name out of the inheritance."

"What?" Billy jumped up and began to swing his arms around wildly. "What are you saying?"

"Daddy loved you like a son, Billy, but your gambling has always worried him. To protect me he has taken you out of the will. Even though we are married, you will have to ask me about every cent you are about to spend after Daddy's gone." She sniffled slightly at the mere thought.

Billy's mouth opened. Charmayne expected a scream, but no sound came forth. At last he dropped himself back on the couch and hung his head in between his knees. "It's not fair," he whined. "How am I going to ever pay off my debts if you and Abe don't bail me out?"

Charmayne shrugged her shoulders. "How about getting a job?"

～

The phone rang.

Charmayne reached for her phone. As she glanced at the screen, her face lit up. It was Molly Gertrude Grey's number. "Miss Grey," she cooed with happy delight. "Is there anything you found out?"

"Maybe," came the reply. "I just want to know about your Daddy's dentist. What was his name?"

"That's a strange question," Charmayne replied. "It was Tyler Florey. He's been our dentist for as long as I can remember."

"And he lives in Calmhaven, right?"

"Yes," Charmayne replied, "of course. In fact, he lives right down the street." She did not understand the validity of the question.

"How about a dentist by the name of Salvatore Swaggart? Did you ever hear of him?"

Charmayne thought for a moment, then broke out into a chuckle. "Sounds more like an opera singer than a dentist. Never heard of him. I don't think there's a dentist by that name in Calmhaven."

"That's right," Molly Gertrude answered. "That man lives in Trenton Valley, fifty miles up north."

"Oh? And what is the connection to my Daddy?" Charmayne narrowed her eyes as she pressed the phone closer to her ear.

"I don't know yet, Charmayne. I am trying to find out," Molly Gertrude replied. "I wish I could tell you more."

Charmayne closed her eyes for a moment. Poor Daddy. How she missed his familiar smile. "Thank you Miss Grey," she said at last. "Call me as soon as you know more."

"I will," Molly Gertrude replied. "Don't you worry now. We'll do the best we can. How is Abe? Any news?"

"Not yet, Miss Molly. Daddy's still not responding.

"Oh, my dear, don't fret. The good Lord will raise him up I am certain. We are praying for you all, you know."

"Thank you, Miss Grey."

"Bye Charmayne."

The conversation was over, and as Charmayne turned her mobile phone off she let out a deep sigh. Life could be very complicated at times.

A VISIT TO TRENTON VALLEY

Early the next morning, Dora turned the key in her Kia Rio, let it run for some time to get the juices flowing and waited until Molly Gertrude was ready to go. When Molly Gertrude had fastened her seatbelt and gave her a gentle nod, she drove off.

They would be visiting Trenton Valley, and more specific, the dental clinic of Salvatore Swaggart. Molly Gertrude had contacted the office and made an appointment for Dora to get her teeth checked.

"I don't need my teeth to get checked," Dora had objected, while she wrinkled her nose. "I just went a few months ago to Tyler Florey." A victorious smile appeared as she lifted up her right index finger and waved it around. "No cavities."

"I would gladly sit in the dentist's chair," Molly Gertrude

explained, "but I've got dentures, so there's no reason for me to make an appointment."

"You pay the bill," Dora had grunted.

Molly Gertrude couldn't help but smile. "Sure, Dora. Expenses are on me."

As they left Calmhaven and took a turn-off to highway 59 that was leading towards Trenton Valley, Dora wanted to know why they actually had to go see Swaggart.

"His business card was in Abe Mortimer's pocket," Molly Gertrude replied. "You told me that JJ Barnes had found it."

Dora shrugged her shoulders. "I have lots of business cards in my house from people I don't even remember."

Molly Gertrude's eyes flashed. "Dora, there's one thing you need to learn…"

"What?"

"There's always a reason for everything. Abe Mortimer has had contact with this Salvatore Swaggart. That card didn't land in his pocket by a strange gust of wind. It may very well be nothing, but in order to solve the mystery, you have to follow up on all possible leads."

Dora nodded without taking her eyes off the road. "You are right, Miss Molly. Of course."

"Charmayne told me that her Daddy always went to Tyler

Flory, just like you. So what's he doing with the address of a dentist 50 miles away from his home?"

"Beats me," Dora said, as she concentrated on overtaking a truck from the Cash'em-Right.

Molly Gertrude pushed the button on the radio, trying to find a station with classical music but when Dora heard a country tune from her favorite band, the Wranglers in Jeans, she cried out and begged Miss Molly to keep the tune playing.

Molly Gertrude didn't particularly like country music but already feeling guilty that she had forced Dora to the dentist chair, she consented. She just had to grin and bear it, and while Dora began to happily sing along, she withdrew from the scene by leaning her head against the window of the Kia Rio.

Baby it's a mystery to me
To understand the misery I see,
But soon I fly to heaven's cloud
And won't be hearing oh, the wicked shout

Yeah-Yeah-Yeah- Time is on our hand
Come and take the stand- Come and take the stand

Dora got quite into the song, and began to drum along by tapping with her left hand on the steering wheel, causing Molly Gertrude to cast nervous glances at the road. But at last the song finally ended, and to Molly Gertrude's relief, she noticed they were nearing the outskirts of Trenton Valley.

"Go slow," Molly Gertrude cautioned. "Trenton Valley is quite a bit bigger than Calmhaven. We don't want to miss the right exit."

"What's the address again?" Dora asked.

"25 Orange Blossom."

"We'll turn here then," Dora suggested as she pointed to an exit sign. "There's a sign for the fruit tree district."

That sounded about right, and indeed, within a few minutes they drove up to Orange Blossom and found Salvatore Swaggart's dental clinic. It was an impressive sight. The clinic was a cubical shaped ultra-modern building with artistic, but apparently meaningless arches on all sides, and was almost entirely made of the type of glass that you could not see through from the outside. A stone path led through a grassy lawn to the entrance and as they walked over it, they passed by a marble statue of an object of fine art. Molly Gertrude stared at it for some time, trying to figure out whether it was a naked man, a handicapped tiger, or possibly an artistic rendition of the artist's worst nightmare. To Molly Gertrude, it was impossible to tell.

But what it *did* show was that Salvatore Swaggart was doing well in his business. This man had cash, that much was clear.

On entering they stepped into the reception area, which was kept spotlessly clean. On the far end, behind a reception desk, sat a young woman properly dressed for the occasion. She wore the uniform of a nurse, her hair was professionally held back in a bun, and a little cap with the name Swaggart embroidered on it adorned her head. She looked up as Molly Gertrude and Dora approached. "Hello," she sang. "May I help you?"

"I've got an appointment to see Doctor Salvatore Swaggart at 11," Dora mumbled.

The lady looked at her computer screen and nodded. "Yes, that's correct. Please sit over there." She pointed to the waiting area a bit hidden from sight. "The doctor will be with you shortly."

She turned back to her work and no longer gave the two women her attention.

Molly Gertrude and Dora sauntered to the waiting area and found a seat.

"This is very different from Tyler Florey's place," Dora whispered to Molly Gertrude, as she picked up a well-worn copy of 'The Way Things Work.' When Molly Gertrude did not answer, she opened the magazine and began to read an article about the mating-procedures of the red wood-ant.

A door opened in the hallway.

Voices came closer, and Molly Gertrude looked up. Dora seemed caught up in her education about ants and did not notice anything. One of the voices sounded familiar. A man appeared around the corner, dressed in a white coat, and a green mask hanging on a string on his chest. He was followed by a round, chubby fellow who was balding.

Molly Gertrude gasped. She knew that person.

There was only one man that looked like that. She grabbed a magazine from the stack in front of her and held it high before her face, so she would not be recognized.

Dora looked up and frowned. "What are you doing, Molly Gertrude?"

"Quiet," Molly Gertrude hissed. "Don't look up. Just keep on reading."

The man in his white coat, Molly Gertrude assumed it was Salvatore Swaggart, shook hands with the other fellow. "Take care, Mr. Finney. Have a good ride back to Calmhaven."

Now Dora realized what was happening and a slight tremor went through her body. There, shaking hands with Salvatore Swaggart, fifty miles away from Calmhaven, stood cake maker Albert Finney.

Both Molly Gertrude and Dora peered over the edge of their magazines and saw how Swaggart handed Finney a brown envelope that was stuffed with something. "Remember, Finney..." Swaggart still said, "... only use these when you absolutely have to, and you see no other way."

Albert Finney nodded and his familiar, shifty smile appeared. "I won't Doctor."

Then he turned and left.

Relief washed over Molly Gertrude. Albert Finney had not seen them. That would have complicated matters unnecessarily. But what was Finney doing here in Trenton Valley, while there was a perfectly good dentist in Calmhaven?

She would have to figure it out later as the man in the white coat walked up to them and asked in a questioning voice, "I am looking for Miss Dora Brightside?"

"That's me," Dora said, as she put her biology lesson on the love life of the red wood-ant back on the table and got up. "Just need a check-up."

Salvatore Swaggart let his dark, green eyes rest on Dora. He seemed to be assessing her. Molly Gertrude did the same, trying not to be too obvious, as she peered at the man by tilting her head and at the same time still pretending to be reading her magazine. But one thing was immediately crystal clear to Molly Gertrude. She did *not* like this man.

He stood before them as if he were a five-star General ready to command his ignorant troupes and was about to send them as cannon-fodder into battle. His smile was clearly pretend, just business and cold. It reminded Molly Gertrude of the way Doctor Francesco Fish had been looking at her when she was just a young child and he had removed her tonsils, cool, professionally and without the least bit of sincere empathy. To such men, patients were just a means to support all kinds of ungodly habits and extravagant life-styles. Thankfully, she had met many a good doctor since that first experience as a child, but when she saw Salvatore Swaggart it was as if an old drawer was opened in her memory bank, and it did not feel very good.

"You are coming here, all the way from Calmhaven?" the dentist asked, his voice grim.

"Yes… eh," Dora replied, not knowing what else to say. "That's right. I am from Calmhaven."

"Why don't you go to that clinic over there?"

Molly Gertrude kept her eyes glued to her magazine, but she felt her blood beginning to boil. Was this some kind of interrogation?

"A man just had an unfortunate accident in town," Molly Gertrude heard Dora answer. "I am the superstitious kind, and prefer not to get treated in Calmhaven for a while."

Molly Gertrude barely could suppress a chuckle, as she heard Dora's surprising excuse. Would Swaggart buy her excuse? It sounded pretty lame.

"Why not?" the dentist asked at last, as he tilted his head in surprise. "His death had nothing to do with dental work, did it?"

"He's not dead!" Dora protested.

Swaggart's eyes flamed. He was not the kind of man who took kindly to be being contradicted.

"I heard he was rushed to hospital flat on his back?"

Dora shrugged her shoulders. "I don't know. Just what I heard on the grapevine. I am just a simple girl." It seemed best not to divulge anything if she did not have to.

A small laugh curled his lips, but it didn't sound small, happy or kind. "He choked on a cake, Miss Brightside, that's what I read." Swaggart informed her as if he was teaching a second-grader. "He was a greedy man who stuffed his mouth too full of cake. Must have been awful for the groom and the bride to experience such a thing on their wedding day."

Dora looked up. "Did you know the man who, em, died? It sounds as if you know a lot of the details?"

"I read about it in the Trenton Valley Gazette. I heard it happened to… Abe Mortimer?"

"You know him?" Dora asked.

The question seemed to startle Swaggart a bit. "Know him? Of course not. Why should I know a man in Calmhaven?"

Molly Gertrude kept eyes to the magazine, but she was all

ears, and couldn't help but feel a wave of admiration for her assistant Dora. The girl was not about to be put in a corner by this strange dentist.

Dora shrugged her shoulders. "Just a question. So you never met Mr. Mortimer?"

"Of course I did not." Swaggart growled.

"There was a business card in Mr. Mortimer's pocket."

"Says who?"

"The police in Calmhaven."

Swaggart took a step back. "Why do you think that has anything to do with me?"

"It was your business card," Dora fired back. "Why would that man carry your business card in his pocket on the day of his daughter's wedding?"

Swaggart's eyes flashed and he lifted up his right index finger and began to wave it in front of Dora's face. "Who are you?" he hissed.

"I told you, Dora," she answered in a girlish voice. "I am just a simple girl."

"You want your teeth done," Swaggart's voice was cold, impatient and rude. "Then let's go. I've got other patients waiting."

"Thank you," Dora said. "On second thought… I think my teeth are fine."

Swaggart narrowed his eyes. "No, I think your teeth need a little work. I can see right from here that your gums are infected. You have what they call Temporomandibular Jaw Pains, and I am afraid you have a problem with thrush as well. Come on, girl... into the chair you go." He walked over to Dora and took her hand.

That was enough.

Molly Gertrude couldn't pretend any longer. She threw her magazine on the table and slapped the dentist's hand.

"Get your hand off my assistant, you quack."

Swaggart withdrew his hand as if bitten by a snake. "Who are you?" he said as he turned to Molly Gertrude.

"It doesn't matter who I am," Molly Gertrude hissed, "but I have the feeling I will never let my assistant come here for her dental work."

"Suit yourself," Swaggart said as he scowled. "I wish for both of you to leave."

He planted his feet firmly in front of both Molly Gertrude and Dora and pointed to the glass door.

Molly Gertrude forced herself back up on her legs and while heavily leaning on her cane she shook her finger in Swaggart's face. "I've been around for a good many years, you good for nothing medicine man, and I can tell a thing or two about the people in front of me."

They could hear him gnashing his teeth, but while his ears

reddened, Swaggart managed to keep his cool, and all he hissed was: "Out!"

Minutes later Molly Gertrude and Dora were back in Dora's Kia Rio.

Molly Gertrude was actually chuckling while she fastened her seatbelt again. "That was interesting." She eyed Dora who seemed a little white around her lips, and then placed her arm on Dora's shoulder. "You did great, Dora... I admired your fight."

Dora shrugged her shoulders. "I am not sure if I will make a very good detective."

"You are one of the best," Molly Gertrude encouraged her. "And... don't tell me you didn't enjoy this little encounter. Remember it's always the hit dog that howls. That guy is a liar and a cheat." Molly Gertrude shook her head in disgust. "That whole dentist business is just some sort of cover up for only God knows what."

"You think so?" Dora's eyes widened.

"He knows more," Molly Gertrude answered. "He's lying about knowing Abe Mortimer. I could tell by his body language. He got all nervous when you confronted him. That man is a charlatan if I ever saw one."

Dora revved up the engine and began driving. "What was Albert Finney doing here?" she asked without taking her eyes off the road.

"Don't really know," Molly Gertrude pressed her lips together. "But he will have some explaining to do."

Molly Gertrude stared at the radio, but decided to leave it off. The chances of finding good classical music were slim these days and she really couldn't stand another country song. Right then Dora broke through the silence. She sounded a bit nervous.

"Miss Molly?" she asked in a small, soft voice. "I know I don't have thrush... but do you think I may have Temperamental Jaw Disease?"

Molly Gertrude narrowed her eyes. "You mean Temporomandibular Jaw Pains? The stuff that Swaggart was talking about? She shook her head. "Of course you don't have that, Dora. Did Pastor Julian not teach you that the devil is a liar and the father of lies? I think we just met one his servants."

14

MORE SECRETS REVEALED

The first thing Molly Gertrude did the next morning was to follow up on JJ Barnes' request that she contact him. She wasn't entirely certain what to expect. Barnes was not a bad man, but he seemed so concerned about making the right impressions that it made him forget his real job as an officer of the law. As a result he had little eye for important details, especially not if these details would require him to swim against the stream. Since nothing ever happened in Calmhaven anyway, it had never been a problem before. But now it was not helping any, and Molly Gertrude did not look forward to another bawling out.

So when she dialed his number she came prepared. She had gone over every detail of her investigation so far, and had an answer to any question the man could possibly ask her. And then, just before calling, she had said the Lord's

Prayer a few times, in the hopes it would help her stay meek, if the conversation got somewhat heated.

"Hello, Sheriff," she purred, hoping to soften the man's heart. "I heard you wanted to talk to me."

"Yes I did, Miss Grey. Thank you for calling me." *Surprise. He sounds almost gentle.*

"Did you want to talk about my investigation?" Molly Gertrude knew she was stepping on thin ice, but it was best to grab the bull by the horns.

"No, Miss Grey. Not at all." He chuckled. "As you know, I am pretty much convinced you are wasting your time. No, I was calling you for an entirely different matter."

"Oh?"

He cleared his throat and then spoke in lofty tones. "It's my birthday, Miss Grey."

"Your birthday?" Molly Gertrude blurted. "Well look at that… congratulations JJ." *I better make sure I send him a card.*

"Not today," Barnes explained. "My birthday is on Saturday."

Molly Gertrude listened.

"You see, I am giving a party Saturday night. You know, informal… Anybody is welcome. There will be lots of snacks, a bowl of punch… a glass of wine for the daring, some music and a dance."

"I don't dance," Molly Gertrude simpered. "I am in my seventies, JJ."

"I know," Barnes replied. "But I am not inviting you to the party."

Excuse me?

Barnes explained. "I mean, you are welcome of course, but that's not the point. I want you to organize it. I'll even pay you for it."

Molly Gertrude narrowed her eyes. Had she heard correctly? JJ Barnes wanted her to organize his birthday party? At last she asked in a perplexed tone. "I don't understand. I am a wedding planner. Is somebody going to marry too?"

Barnes laughed. "No, Miss Grey. Nobody is going to marry. I'll be honest with you." He waited for impact and then said, "The way you arrange everything is marvelous. My wife always gets so nervous about such things, and I am too busy with my work as a Sheriff."

Molly Gertrude thought it over. "What did you have in mind, Sheriff?"

"I'll send you a list of things I would like to see. But it's going to be really small. If you could arrange a few waiters, good food and the music. Will you do it?"

This was just about the last thing Molly Gertrude had expected, but why not? "Sure, Sheriff. If you could email the details to my office, Miss Brightside and I will get to work."

"Thank you, Miss Grey," Sheriff Barnes gurgled with a small laugh. "I knew I could count on you. And..." his voice trailed off, "... just between you and me, forget about wasting your time on Abe Mortimer's cake calamity. You are a much better party-girl than a detective." His laugh rolled through the phone, as he apparently thought he was quite funny.

After he had closed the connection Molly Gertrude stared for a while at the horn in her hand. She had to admit, this was the last thing she had expected.

As soon as Molly Gertrude met with Dora, later that day, she told her about the invitation she had received from JJ Barnes. She figured Dora would be tickled pink, but instead of an enthusiastic reaction, Dora seemed somewhat uneasy.

Molly Gertrude frowned and added, "I was actually worried JJ Barnes would start lecturing me again. Don't you think it's quite a surprise?"

"Yes, sure," Dora mumbled. "But... well, I can't help on Saturday night."

Molly Gertrude's eyes widened. "How did you know the party is on Saturday night? I didn't tell you that."

"Because..." Dora's voice was barely audible, "... I am already invited to the birthday party... as a guest."

Molly Gertrude stared at Dora while she narrowed her eyes. "You are invited? By who?"

Dora blushed and looked away. "Deputy Digby asked me. He wants me to go with him to the dance."

Molly Gertrude's face lit up. "Isn't that wonderful?" She clapped her hands in jubilation. "I've always thought you and Digby are good for each other."

"Not too fast, Miss Molly," Dora said, "I know that you are matchmaker but my heart is not something I will give away on a whim."

"Sure," Molly Gertrude nodded as she cast Dora a warm smile. "However, I am not so pleased that our gentle deputy is about to steal my assistant away. I am not sure if I can get the work done all by myself."

"Nonsense, Miss Molly," Dora snapped back. "It's only a onetime thing. I am not even sure I like Digby. And as far as the preparations for Saturday night's party, of course, you can count on me. It's just on the evening itself I am going to be busy."

Molly Gertrude nodded. "There should not be a whole lot of preparing to do. Sheriff Barnes assured me it was a very small job, which needed just the bare minimum of preparations. He told me he would send me a list of his wants and needs."

"When?"

Molly Gertrude shrugged her shoulders. "It's probably already in your in-box. Would you mind checking your email. If the list is in, would you mind starting? I have one more little errand to perform."

"Sure." Dora switched on her computer. "Where are you going?"

"I'd like to visit Billy Monroe. There are still some things I need to find out, and then, when I am finished with Billy, maybe you and I can pay Albert Finney one more visit. The man seems as slippery as an eel, but I would like to know what he was doing in Trenton Valley at that dentist's office."

"Will you be careful, Miss Molly," Dora asked, concern in her eyes.

Molly Gertrude laughed. "Am I not always careful? I am just an innocent, old, arthritis ridden Granny. Nobody suspects me to be snooping around."

"I sure hope so," Dora said while she sighed. Then she turned her attention to her computer screen and began to read.

JJ Barnes' list with wants and needs had arrived.

Billy Monroe looked surprised when he opened the mahogany door of the Mortimer estate where he and his new wife were staying, and stared into the smiling face of Molly Gertrude Grey. "Miss Grey," he mumbled, "w-what can I do for you? If you are looking for Charmayne, she's not here. She went to the Cash'em-Right."

Molly Gertrude shook her head. "No Billy. I came for you."

"For me?" Billy repeated, without making a move.

"Do you mind if I come in?"

Billy rubbed his chin as if he were considering his options. Then he squinted his eyes, and asked, "Why? What do you want from me?"

"Not in a good mood, today?" Molly Gertrude asked. As the words flew out of her mouth, she realized it could come across a bit offensive, and she mumbled, "I just wanted to see how you are doing Billy. That's all."

"I am fine," Billy fired back, but by the sadness in his eyes, it was clear he was lying.

"Abe's accident must have been a great shock to you," Molly Gertrude tried again. "He's like a father to you, is he not?" Those words hit a sensitive spot. Billy's eyes glistened and he gave Molly Gertrude a short nod. "How is he?"

"He's still flat on his back, Miss Molly. Charmayne is beside herself with worry. He looks so ill, I get to thinking he may be better off dead."

"Oh my, careful what you say, young Billy. Can we talk, just for a short while?" Molly Gertrude coaxed.

Billy nodded, and as he opened the door all the way he made a welcoming gesture with his hand. "Just for a little while then. I am not feeling too good."

Molly Gertrude entered the house and handed Billy her coat. "I can understand that, Billy."

Billy hung up her coat and sighed. "It's nothing, really Miss Grey. I suppose the whole thing has left me bewildered. I even got into an argument with Charmayne about it."

Without waiting for Molly Gertrude's response he turned and walked toward the living room and sank down in his favorite seat, right near the glassy sliding doors that gave a breathtaking view of the Mortimer's garden.

Molly Gertrude stood in the doorway, not sure if she should sit down as well. "Can I sit, Billy?" she asked at last, as Billy did not seem highly trained in his social skills.

"Suit yourself," Billy replied while he shrugged his shoulders. He seemed depressed.

"So what's wrong with Charmayne?" Molly Gertrude asked after she had lowered herself onto a sturdy living room chair.

Billy arched his brow. "Charmayne is mad at me."

"I am sad to hear that," Molly Gertrude consoled. "I

suppose, the wedding cake disaster has not helped the start of your marriage very much."

"You can say that," Billy grumbled. "Did you hear?"

"What?"

"I am no longer in Abe's will."

Molly Gertrude looked up. That was news. "What do you mean?"

"Can I be much clearer?" Billy snapped back. "Abe Mortimer took me out of the will. I don't get a red cent of Mortimer's money. It all goes to Charmayne."

Molly Gertrude thought about Billy's words. "I don't see a problem. You two are married. You are even living in the Mortimer's estate," Molly consoled, "And don't write old Abe off yet – he may be laid flat now but if the town's prayers have any sway he'll be up and fighting with twice the fire he had before all of this unfortunate mess."

Billy looked up, anger written all over his face. "She won't pay my debts. Imagine that… she says I need to find a job, and she claims, I haven't been honest with her. But I believe she's still having fancy times with Albert Finney behind my back. She's not honest with me."

Molly Gertrude forced herself to keep a straight face. He really was, as Papa Julian had said, a big, immature baby that still needed to have his spiritual diapers changed now and then. "Maybe it's time to count your blessings."

"What blessings?"

Molly Gertrude shook her head. "For one, you are married to one of the kindest women I know. You live in a mansion, and Abe Mortimer forgave you your sins."

"Yeah," Billy said with a scowl. "I am a blessed man full of debts. I am so blessed that my gentle wife is forcing me to take on a slave job."

Molly Gertrude had always considered herself to be a patient woman, but she decided it was time to turn up the heat a little. "Did you know Billy that you are a possibly a suspect in a possible murder case?"

Billy's eyes widened. "Me? That's preposterous. What murder case?"

"The death of your father-in-law, Abe Mortimer. If Abe doesn't make it you will be top of the list! There are people who think you actually may have tried to kill Abe Mortimer, hoping to get the inheritance. I shouldn't be saying this, but there's an investigation going on."

A shock went through Billy's slender frame. "The police are investigating me? Who told you that?"

"I can't tell you, Billy, but things do not look good. After all, you forced that cake on your father-in-law and you have big gambling debts."

Billy jumped up out of his seat. "I-I...," he stammered, "I loved Abe. I didn't try to kill him. He-he just choked on too much cake and cream!"

A guttural, subterranean howl erupted from his throat

and he began to wring his hands while staring with fearful eyes at Molly Gertrude. "You have to believe me, Miss Grey. Abe is like a father to me. It's true that I was hoping to get rid of my debts, but I was just going to ask Abe for a loan. He would have given the money without question."

"But you have a history of crime, don't you, Billy?"

"Me?" Billy forced his lips into a smile and a nervous giggle rolled out his mouth. "I have no record."

"That's right," Molly Gertrude put on the screws. "But only because Abe Mortimer did not press charges after you broke into his house. Why did you break into his house when you were a teenager, Billy?"

Another spasm of pain flashed over Billy's face. "You know about that?"

Molly Gertrude simply nodded.

"I did not know Abe at the time. I did not know he was a good man." He hissed and pointed to the richly decorated living room. "Look at all the wealth. We thought it would be easy to steal from him."

"Who is we, Billy?"

"My friend George and I."

"George who?"

"George Latimer. He was only 13 or 14 at the time. Just a kid I had befriended."

"What happened to George?" Molly Gertrude wanted to know.

Billy shook his head. "I don't know. After we were caught stealing, Abe dropped the charges against us and took me under his wing. I believe George was sent to Trenton Valley, to some sort of youth facility. I've never seen him since."

"What did he look like?"

Billy smacked his lips. "What does a thirteen-year-old kid look like? Kids all look alike."

"Do you still have an old picture or something?|

Billy shrugged. "I've got one. Actually, it belongs to Charmayne. It's in her family album."

"Can I see it?"

Billy scratched his forehead. "Sure." He got up and walked over to a small antique cupboard in the corner, pulled out a drawer, and rummaged around for some time. At last he returned, hauling a heavy red-leather photo album under his arm. He placed it before Molly Gertrude on the coffee table, turned a few pages and pointed to an old photograph, partly bleached out by the sun and very grainy. The picture portrayed a smiling Abe Mortimer who had his arm slung around another man, who was smiling too, while holding up some sort of image, a tiny sculpture of some kind.

"That's Abe Mortimer and another fellow. That's not George." Molly Gertrude raised her eyebrows.

"Look in the background," Billy clarified. "And indeed, in the back, standing in the shade, were two boys. One was Billy, and the other one...

"That's George," Billy mumbled as he placed his finger on the boy. "I told you, it's hard to see, and that picture was taken over ten years ago."

Molly Gertrude peered at the boy. Dora had told her that with today's technology they could do wonders in enhancing old photographs, but she doubted Calmhaven's police force possessed such devices. George was indeed just a kid, but there was something strange about his features. "He looks... different," Molly Gertrude mumbled without being able to exactly point out what was the matter with George.

"George was sick." Billy seemed to have guessed Molly Gertrude's concerns. "It's partly the quality of the photo, but he did not look too good. He had some sort of immune disease."

"Poor boy," Molly Gertrude mumbled. Then she looked up and asked, "What is the occasion for this picture?"

"Abe and this other fellow were helping troubled kids. Boys like me and George. They received some sort of reward for doing good that day." He shrugged his shoulders. "Abe deserved that reward, but I didn't like the other fellow. He was a big, fat phony."

"Oh?" Molly Gertrude looked up. "What happened to him?"

"I don't know," Billy said and shook his head. "He's some kind of doctor. He left town years ago."

"Name?"

Billy rubbed his nose and thought. "Willy... Willy Wilmot."

Molly Gertrude studied Wilmot. The man in the photograph was clearly tickled pink for having received the honorary reward, and he stood in front of the camera like a victorious warlord, stately, proud and untouchable, as if he was God's good gift to humanity. His demeanor reminded Molly Gertrude of somebody, but she could not quite place her finger on it. The man's hair was way too long, unkempt and wild and hung over his ears, just in the style of that day. He had an enormous toothpaste smile, but his teeth seemed in immaculate condition. "Can I take this picture?" she asked at last. "I'll return it in good condition."

Billy shrugged his shoulders. "Sure, as long as I won't get in trouble with Charmayne. I am already in the dog house."

Molly Gertrude nodded and gently lifted the photograph from the page.

Billy sank down in his seat again and began another round of moans. "You have to believe me, Miss Grey. I had nothing to do with the cake fiasco, honest. It really was an accident."

"I don't believe it was, Billy," Molly Gertrude said while she fastened her eyes on Billy. "I too believe someone wanted Abe Mortimer dead."

Billy let out a sob and he yelled in a high-pitched voice. "It wasn't me, Miss Grey. You must believe me. I loved Abe."

Molly Gertrude nodded. "Maybe, Billy. God knows what really happened that day, and I believe we will all know soon," she said in a decisive voice. "You want my advice?"

He looked up, hope covering his face.

"Get serious about the chances that life is giving you. You are blaming everyone else for your trouble, but there's only one person responsible, and that is you, yourself."

"It's difficult," Billy moaned.

"Of course, it is," Molly Gertrude coached, "but there are people who can help you. There's Papa Julian, and Charmayne loves you."

"She's just mad," Billy blubbered.

"And rightfully so," Molly Gertrude fired back. "You've been dishonest with her. You've only been married for a week and you've already caused serious strain in your marriage. That's probably a new record."

Molly Gertrude's words were like a hammer, nailing down the truth that Billy had been fighting for so long, and he gave her a helpless stare. But Molly Gertrude was done and got up. "Thank you for your time Billy. Next time I'll take tea with one spoon of sugar, and a cookie."

Billy stared at her not understanding, but Molly Gertrude did not want to wait any longer and extended her hand. Billy, with a lame expression, shook it, after which Molly Gertrude let herself out. Papa Julian was right. Maybe Billy was not a bad boy at heart, and Molly Gertrude highly doubted he had anything to do with the suspicious circumstances surrounding Abe's predicament. But he sure was a big baby and if he wasn't careful his relationship with Charmayne would end before it had even had a chance to start.

15

SLEUTHING AT PORTMAN ROAD

The visit with Billy had not yielded any new information, but it had strengthened Molly Gertrude in her conviction that most likely, Billy had nothing to do with the whole affair. He was just a misguided kid, and he had his problems, but he did not strike her as a cruel killer.

But Albert Finney was altogether a different story... and what was the role of that dentist Swaggart in Trenton Valley, if any? It was also disconcerting that they had not been able to find out more about Bald-Head. What was that man doing with his wigs and false moustaches? When Molly Gertrude had fled his house that night, she had written down his exact address, and Dora had made a short call to Deputy Digby, hoping he would be able to tell them who lived there. But there had been no satisfying results.

"Hello, Digby." Dora had called. "Can you do me a favor? I

need to know who lives at 6 Portman Road."

"What's that?" Digby had answered.

"It's a street in Waterside Snomp. Molly Gertrude is wondering who lives there?"

"Ah," Digby exclaimed, as now he understood. "I'll call you back."

And he did.

Three minutes later.

"6 Portman Road," he said, "is owned by a man in New York, called Gregory Duff, but he seems to be renting it out. There's no record of who is living there at the moment." He chuckled. "Waterside Snomp is not a very pleasant part of Calmhaven. I hope you aren't thinking of buying the property?"

"No, Digby," Dora answered, "It's just part of Molly Gertrude's investigation."

"Fine," Digby replied. Then he changed the subject. "Can't wait till Saturday night."

Dora giggled. "See you on Saturday. And thank you for your help."

After she closed the call, she informed Molly Gertrude. "Nothing. There's no record of who is living there at the moment."

Molly Gertrude shrugged her shoulders. "Doesn't matter. We'll just keep plowing ahead and something will turn up sooner or later. It's time to go see Albert Finney. I wonder if we can garner a bit more information out of him."

Minutes later the Kia Rio drove off again, and Dora carefully guided her whoopty through the streets of Calmhaven. Just when she wanted to take a left in order to take the direction for Waterside Snomp, Molly Gertrude raised both of her hands in the air and blurted out, "Stop!"

Dora gave her an angry stare as she slowed down. "Whoa, nothing like a good scare while driving the car. What's wrong?"

"Sorry," Molly Gertrude apologized. "It's just that we passed by Tilly's, and I am out of cat food." She turned her head and pointed backwards. "Would you mind turning around and driving to her store?"

Tilly's was a small supermarket and she sold whatever essentials the locals needed. For the bigger items she had to direct her customers to the Cash'em-Right or even to another town altogether, but over the years Tilly had accumulated all sorts of weird and wonderful items, alongside the more simple groceries such as milk, eggs and bread, and, of course, Misty's favorite cat food.

Dora pressed her lips together and shrugged. "Sure, but why not go to the Cash'em-Right. Tilly's is expensive."

"And she is *good*." Molly Gertrude narrowed her eyes. "Misty only eats stuff from Tilly's. The Cash'em-Right is just one of those ungodly chain stores. I never go down there unless I absolutely have to."

"No problem," Dora said. She checked in her rearview mirror and when the coast was clear she made a U-turn.

When Molly Gertrude entered a few minutes later, a loud bell, attached right above the door, announced her arrival. The store was empty, but while Molly Gertrude loaded several cans of Feline Delight in her shopping cart, Tilly appeared. She was a bubbly, enthusiastic woman with hair that was tucked hurriedly back in a bun. Tilly had a radiant face to match her lively personality. Some folks claimed her mouth was way too big. At first Molly Gertrude had not understood what these people meant, as Tilly's mouth seemed fine. But it had not taken long to find out. Tilly loved a good story, especially a scandal, and her mouth was constantly flapping open and closed, while at the same time prying out the latest tales of Calmhaven's rich and famous. (Calmhaven hardly had any rich, let alone any famous, but that didn't stop Tilly from blabbering all the latest anyway). Tilly certainly had a good heart, but she was easily led to share any juicy tidbits that happened upon her ears.

When Molly Gertrude placed the cat food on the counter and Tilly totaled it up, she gave Molly Gertrude one of her huge smiles.

Molly Gertrude knew she was about to be drawn into one of Tilly's long-winded, gossipy stories. "I saw a man today," Tilly said in a serious voice, as if that was something that hardly ever happened in Calmhaven. She tilted her head back in order to heighten the effect of her statement.

"I did too," Molly Gertrude replied. In her mind's eye she saw a picture of Billy Monroe again. *Poor, immature Billy Monroe.*

"You don't understand," Tilly bubbled. "I *really* saw a man. A nice man." She lowered her voice. "Rich… He smelled like money. And… he's a professional."

"That's wonderful," Molly Gertrude said politely, hoping to get her cat food so she could leave."

"I've been *praying* for a dentist," Tilly went on, still whispering. As she said the word 'dentist' a shiver went through Molly Gertrude's spine. "What did you say, Tilly?"

Tilly giggled. "Now you are getting interested, Molly Gertrude. But you are too old for this man."

"What man?" Molly Gertrude urged.

"A dentist from Trenton Valley. Such a nice fellow." Tilly folded her arms and stared at the heavens. Actually, she stared at the ceiling, but it was clear she was having visions of something that reached much further than her ceiling.

"What was his name?" Molly Gertrude was all ears.

"No-no-no," Tilly shook her finger. "I met him first."

Molly Gertrude was about to lose her patience and considered getting irate, but she knew that wasn't going to help any, so she swallowed her irritation, and replied in as sweet a voice as she could muster, "Just curious, Tilly. I am no competition, I assure you."

Tilly smiled. "Of course you are not. I know," she nodded. Then she pulled out a business card. Molly Gertrude's eyes grew wide. It was from Salvatore Swaggart.

"His name is Swaggart," Tilly affirmed.

"Why was he here?"

"He was asking for an address," Tilly replied. "You see, the poor man was lost. Apparently, his car doesn't have a GPS."

"What address?" Molly Gertrude almost shouted it out.

"6 Portman Road," came Tilly's answer. "That's very close to here, so I told him how to get there. He told me he may be back and then he'll take me for dinner." A hopeful giggle erupted from Tilly's mouth.

"Thanks, Tilly," Molly Gertrude cried out. She opened her purse, pulled out a five dollar bill and slammed it on the counter, right next to the cat food. Then she grabbed her cans and turned around in order to leave.

"You still get change," Tilly called out.

"Never mind," Molly Gertrude called back without turning as she shuffled out the door as fast as she could. There was not a minute to waste. They needed to go down to Portman Road first. Finney just had to wait.

"Dora," she called out already as she was approaching the car. "Change of plans. Please drive to 6 Portman Road."

"To that ugly place again?" Dora wrinkled her nose.

"That's right," Molly Gertrude blurted. "And hurry."

$\sim$

Dora parked her Kia Rio again at the same spot as before. The light was now very different from when they had been there in the evening. The glare of the sun was quite bright, and unlike the other time, there were several customers at the Cash'em-Right who were pushing their shopping carts around.

Molly Gertrude assessed the situation. "Staying here will not help us any. Let's walk over to Bald-Head's house again. Of course, we need to be careful, since Swaggart has seen us in Trenton Valley, but nothing ventured, nothing gained."

Dora agreed, and both women climbed out of the car. After Dora had locked her doors, they walked again in the direction of the house.

"What exactly do you hope to accomplish?" Dora whispered while they were walking down the street. "We can't very well just ring the bell and ask Swaggart what he is doing here."

"I don't know, Dora," Molly Gertrude replied. "We can only try, try, and try some more. If we are faithfully checking up on all leads and possibilities, we may eventually stumble upon the right puzzle piece." She chuckled. "Sleuthing women need lots of patience, Dora. Lots."

"I guess so," Dora mumbled back, but she did not sound convinced.

"You know how many times Thomas Edison failed in inventing the light bulb?" Molly Gertrude went on in a cheerful voice.

Dora shrugged her shoulders. "I don't know. Ten times, maybe?"

"Wrong," Molly Gertrude said with a laugh. "Almost a thousand times. You see, Dora, victory belongs to the most persevering."

"At least Edison knew what he was looking for," Dora objected. They were now almost at the house.

A shiny, blue Corvette was parked in front of the rusty gate of the house of Bald-Head. One of its front tires was carelessly parked on the sidewalk. A strange sight, to see such an expensive car in front of the dilapidated building.

"Y-You think, that car belongs to Swaggart?" Dora whispered as she let her fingers slide over the hood.

"It has to be," Molly Gertrude replied. "I am going in."

"What?" Dora's face paled.

Molly Gertrude pointed to the other side of the street, to

a cement electrical building. "You hide behind there, and wait for me. If I am not back in say 15 minutes, you call Digby."

"But… what are you going to do?"

"The garage door is still open. There's light enough. I am going in, hoping to find out more."

Dora shook her head. "Miss Molly Gertrude Grey, you are absolutely crazy! You are *not* going to do it."

Molly Gertrude's eyes widened. "You are not going to try to stop me, are you?"

"I am," Dora replied. "I will go in your stead. And you are the one that's going to hide behind that slab of cement."

Molly Gertrude gasped. "A-Are you sure, Dora… I thought you would be a little scared."

"I am," Dora fired back. "But don't talk me out of this. If I let you go in, stumbling around with your aching joints, leaning on a walking cane, we are sure to get caught. I'll do it. Just wish me luck."

"Come here, Dora," Molly Gertrude said.

Dora tilted her head, not understanding why Molly Gertrude asked her to come over.

"I need to give you a hug," Molly Gertrude whispered. "I am proud of you. Snooping around brings out the best in you."

Never before had the minutes gone by so slow for Molly Gertrude. Her hushed prayers for Dora's safety wafted heavenward as she did her best to survey the house for any signs of a scuffle.

She had positioned herself behind the small cement building. Deciding not to get annoyed by the constant buzzing sound coming from the generators, there was nothing else to do but wait. Dear Dora had amazed her.

Molly Gertrude had not *really* wanted to go in, knowing full well she was not able to move as stealthily as was necessary for such an undertaking. But, there had been no alternative. Dora had been acting a bit scared before, and she could not subject Dora to such adventures. But apparently, the lioness that had been lying dormant within Dora's heart had been awakened, and the girl was well on her way to becoming a trustworthy detective.

But why was she taking so long?

Molly Gertrude glanced around the wall of the cement building again. Everything seemed still. Nothing moved. No sound was heard.

But just as Molly Gertrude pulled her head back, there was a sound. The front door of Bald-Head's house opened and Swaggart appeared. His bulky soldier frame stepped out onto the porch. He seemed agitated, nervous and hard. He turned around and shook his finger at someone who was not visible. It was impossible to hear his words, but right then the face of Bald-Head appeared in the doorway.

The man laughed, although laughing was really not the right word. He snickered and mocked, and pointed to the shiny Corvette, as if to signify that Swaggart needed to leave. The more Molly Gertrude saw of Bald-Head, the more convinced she was that she had seen him before.

The dentist too seemed more familiar than he had before.

Swaggart descended the steps of the porch, and hurried off to his car. Just before he stepped inside, he turned around and waved his fist in the air. "I am warning you... You are playing with fire."

"So are you, Wilmot," Bald-Head cried out in a loud, angry voice.

Wilmot? Why did Bald-Head call Swaggart by that name? Molly Gertrude's heart skipped a beat. Had she heard correctly?

Swaggart started his engine and drove off with screeching tires. Bald-Head stared after the car for a while, and when Swaggart had disappeared around the corner, he stepped back into his house and slammed the door closed.

Where was Dora?

Molly Gertrude peered around the corner again... No sign of her yet.

Dear God, bring Dora out safely.

Then, to Molly Gertrude's great relief, she saw Dora sneak out of the garden. Good girl... she had not gotten herself caught.

The gate creaked again as Dora came out, and seconds later the two women stared at each other with relieved and joyful faces.

"D-did you hear what Bald-Head called Swaggart?" Molly Gertrude whispered, barely able to keep her voice down. "He called him Wilmot."

Dora frowned. She did not understand.

Molly Gertrude grabbed her purse and fished out the picture Billy had given her and pointed to Willy Wilmot. "Recognize this fellow? I thought he looked familiar..."

As Dora stared at the picture her eyes widened. "That's Swaggart," she confirmed.

"That's right," Molly Gertrude hissed. "Swaggart knows Abe Mortimer. They were buddies before. Billy told me all about this picture."

Dora took the picture again out of Molly Gertrude's hand and studied it some more. Then she shook her head and looked up at Molly Gertrude, her eyes round and big. "And that boy we know too," she gasped as she pointed at the boy in the background next to Billy Monroe. "That is..." Dora paused for a moment in silenced disbelief, "Bald-Head!"

"What?" Molly Gertrude grabbed the picture out of Dora's

hand and stared at it again. "Are you sure? How can you tell? It's a bad picture."

Dora pressed her lips together. "I know it's one and the same. And it's confirmed by what I heard inside, and by what Billy told you about this man."

"What did you hear?"

"Let's not stay here," Dora suggested. "We'll talk in the car. I am not feeling very comfortable behind this slab of cement, right near the house of a would-be killer."

"Good idea," Molly Gertrude replied. She glanced around the corner again to see if the coast was clear. Then, both women walked with a steady pace away from 6 Portman Road to the safety of Dora's Kia Rio.

16

RATTLING ALBERT FINNEY

"So," Molly Gertrude asked as she and Dora had climbed back into their car. "What did you hear?"

"An argument. Swaggart was furious." Dora chuckled. "It was child's play getting in the garage and these two fellows were so mad that they were shouting at each other. Thus, overhearing what they said was a piece of cake too, no pun intended."

"What were they arguing about?"

"I demand respect," Dora mimicked Swaggart's dark voice. "After all I have done for you, you treat me like this? I took care of you and that miserable Billy when you were just castaways; waifs without a future. But I helped you."

And listen to what Bald-Head then answered. "If I am going down, you're going down with me. You always wanted me to do your dirty work... but I am sick and tired of the way you've been treating me." Molly Gertrude couldn't help but giggle, as Dora's voice matched Bald-Head's to a tee. "Look at the place I am staying at, while you live in wealth and luxury. How dare you even show up here in that stupid Corvette of yours!"

"They were at each other's throats," Dora concluded. "There was more talk about JJ Barnes going to arrest both of them, but I could hear no more, as Swaggart ran out the door."

Molly Gertrude leaned back in her seat and closed her eyes for a moment, as she thought things over. "Things are getting much clearer, Dora," she mumbled without opening her eyes. "You know, I always told you I had the feeling I met Bald-Head somewhere before?

"And?" Dora asked.

"I think I've got an idea." She opened her eyes. "Let me muse over it for some time. I still want to talk to Charmayne as well..." Then she changed the subject and asked, "But, weren't we on our way to Albert Finney?"

"We were," Dora agreed.

"Then let's go there," Molly Gertrude thought out loud. "There is still much that is unclear. What did Finney do at Swaggart's dental clinic? And why did he get that strange, brown envelope... What's his connection to all this?"

Dora snorted. "I have no idea."

"Then let's find out," Molly Gertrude eyes lit up like two,

adventurous little lights. "I'll talk to Finney, and you excuse yourself while there."

"What do you mean?"

Molly Gertrude shrugged her shoulders. "Tell him you ate something bad and your stomach is upset. While I am keeping Finney busy, you do some more sleuthing and see if you can come up with something, anything really, that ties Finney to this case. I don't think I want to confront him straight out with his visit to Trenton Valley. It may be too early for that. "

Dora chuckled. "This is getting exciting, Miss Molly."

"Life is exciting, child," Molly Gertrude exclaimed. "You just have not discovered that yet."

When they drove up to Albert Finney's place, to Molly Gertrude's relief, they saw his Toyota sitting in the drive way. Albert Finney was home. But they did not receive a warm welcome. The man was not pleased in the least to see Molly Gertrude and Dora again.

"I am busy. Extremely busy," he almost shouted out when he opened the door and saw who it was that was standing on his porch. "I will not let you in."

"Oh," Molly Gertrude said, greatly disappointed. "Actually, I don't need to come in at all."

"You don't?"

Molly Gertrude shook her head. "No, I don't. But I would like to ask for your expertise about cars. I am afraid there's a terrible, rattling noise under the hood, and Dora and I have a long journey ahead of us."

"So? What does that have to do with me?" A big scowl hung over Finney's face.

"We were just driving by," Molly Gertrude spoke in a sheepish voice, "when we heard that strange rattling noise."

"And?"

"Well, the nearest garage is at least a two-mile drive, and we saw your house. I know you are a real gentleman…" she lowered her eyes. "Would you please help two damsels in distress, and at least take a look at the motor, to see if it's safe enough to continue on our journey?"

At that moment, Dora cringed and made a painful sound.

Finney turned his head. "What's wrong with you?" he barked.

"I don't know," Dora stammered. "Something I ate, I presume… May I use your bathroom for a moment?"

Albert Finney wrinkled his nose. He clearly had no mind to help, but he did have a name to uphold. He shook his head in disgust and made room for Dora to enter. "Second door to the right."

"In the meantime I'll show you the car," Molly Gertrude

said, and without waiting for Albert's reply, she turned and walked towards the Kia Rio.

Albert looked helpless, and followed her like a dog who had just gotten a beating.

"Here's the car," Molly Gertrude said.

"I can see that," Albert Finney croaked. "Of course you have problems with this clunker."

"Why, Mr. Finney?"

"Because it's as old as the Garden of Eden," Finney whined.

Molly Gertrude frowned. "Adam and Eve didn't have a Kia Rio, Mr. Finney."

Finney cast her an angry stare. "Do you think I am stupid, Miss Grey. It's a saying… a smart saying to indicate that this car is a piece of trash."

Molly Gertrude acted hurt. "It still drives, Mr. Finney. Let me open the hood."

She opened the car door and felt with her fingers under the dashboard for the handle with which she could open the hood. After she had felt around for some time, she stuck her head out of the car again and said with a tired voice. "Can't find it, Mr. Finney. Would you take a look?"

Finney growled. His patience was sorely being tried. "Get out of the way, old lady."

"Sure." Molly Gertrude moved aside as Finney searched for the handle. Seconds later the hood sprang open.

"Do you see anything wrong?" Molly Gertrude asked.

"There's nothing to see," Finney fired back. "The motor is not running."

"Ah... I see," Molly Gertrude said. "Then I guess, I will have to turn on the motor."

"Yes," Finney growled, grinded his teeth. "That may be a good idea."

Molly Gertrude opened her purse and began to rummage around. She looked up and cast Finney an apologetic smile. "I am sorry, Mr. Finney... a woman's handbag is like a jungle sometimes. We women have to carry loads of stuff around."

"Whatever," Finney replied while tapping his foot on the pavement.

"Oops," Molly Gertrude cried out after she had been searching for several minutes. "I don't have the key." She cast Finney a weary smile. "You see, this is actually Miss Brightside's car. I thought she had given the key to me, but I suppose she still has it in her bag."

Finney was done. He was finished. "What utter nonsense," he cried. "I've lost enough time already. Good day, Miss Grey."

He turned and walked back to the house, and Molly Gertrude could almost see the angry clouds of fury rise up out of his head. She desperately wanted to keep him near the car, but her reservoir of tricks had been exhausted. But then, and to Molly Gertrude's great relief, Dora stepped out of the house, onto the porch.

"Thank you, for letting me use your bathroom, Mr. Finney... I feel so much better." Then she asked in a cheerful voice, "Is the car all right?"

"I would not know," Finney blurted out in passing, "And frankly, I don't care." The cake maker let out another growl, hopped onto his porch, and after he had entered his house, he slammed the door closed.

"Nice man," Molly Gertrude commented as she noticed the door was still shaking on its hinges. She turned to Dora. "I am so glad you made it out of there on time. You probably didn't find anything."

"As a matter of fact," Dora cooed, "I did," Her face shone. "But before we talk, let's move away from here, I don't like the idea of that man staring at us through the window."

Molly Gertrude agreed, and soon they drove away from the Finney house.

"I found that brown envelope." Dora began as soon as she felt free enough to talk.

Molly Gertrude stared at her. "You *did*? Where?"

"In the bathroom. There was aspirin in the envelope."

Molly Gertrude tilted her head, not quite understanding what Dora said. "What do you mean?"

Dora cast her a quick glance. "Aspirin... the stuff you take when you have a headache."

"I know what aspirin is," Molly Gertrude snorted, "but why would Swaggart give that to Finney?"

Dora shrugged her shoulders while steering her car towards Molly Gertrude's house. "I don't know. There were several full boxes of aspirin in there. Two empty ones too."

Molly Gertrude scratched her head. "Why would he need so much aspirin?"

"I don't know," Dora commented. "Maybe he drinks too much. You should see his stash of liquor. I bet he is well-acquainted with the effects of a hangover."

Molly Gertrude discarded the idea. "I don't think so. He got this from Swaggart, and that man is a dentist." Molly Gertrude closed her eyes. She usually did that when she really wanted to think.

"Aspirin is not only for headaches," she mumbled. "Some doctors prescribe it to help prevent the risk of a stroke, while I've heard it being used as a heart regimen as well."

She tapped her finger on the dashboard. "I am going to do a bit more research about this."

"Sure," Dora said, trying to be helpful. "But can I ask you something else?"

"Of course."

"That party for Saturday night… It needs our attention. There are still some decisions to make. Sheriff Barnes sent us a list of people he would like us to invite. Furthermore, we need to hire a few waiters, buy snacks, drinks and we need to decorate the place. Finally, we still need to arrange for a live-band or a DJ."

"That's a lot of work," Molly Gertrude agreed.

"My point," Dora quipped. "We may need to put this investigation on the back burner. After all, we need the income too."

Molly Gertrude's face lit up. "Great. Let's divide the chores."

"Good," Dora answered.

"I'll hire the waiters, and I will send out the invitations," Molly Gertrude said in a decisive voice. "If you can give me the list of all the people that were hired for the wedding, then I can see if I can hire a few of the same characters. You handle the rest."

Dora frowned. "But then, my job is way bigger than yours."

Molly Gertrude smiled. "Just trust me, Dora. Just get this show on the road for Saturday, and I will do those two things I said I would."

Dora glanced for a moment at Molly Gertrude. "You are up to something, aren't you?" she finally spoke.

"Someone tried to murder Abe Mortimer," Molly

Gertrude replied. "I am sure of it, and now I think I know what happened. I still have to talk to Charmayne, but I think we can solve this whole mystery right at JJ Barnes' birthday party." She chuckled. "That way he gets to take the credit for it as well. And since that is so important to him, it should make him feel good."

They had just reached Molly Gertrude's street.

"Thank you for all your incredible help, Dora," Molly Gertrude said as she unscrewed her way out of Dora's car. "Make sure you get a good night's sleep."

"I will, Miss Molly. You too. Good night."

"Good night, Dora. See you tomorrow."

17

THE BIRTHDAY PARTY

The next morning, Molly Gertrude called Charmayne and arranged to see her at the Cozy Bridal Agency. Molly Gertrude did not want to take a chance of running into Billy again, and it turned out Charmayne was happy to leave the house.

"Coming to the office is fine, Miss Grey," Charmayne explained. "I am already scheduled to meet some friends at Marmelotte's Tearoom later today, so I am already in town anyway." Then she asked the question that was foremost on her mind. "Do you have any news?"

"Maybe," Molly Gertrude replied. "There are a few things I would like to ask you, but I would rather not jump to conclusions. Talking to you may clear up a lot of the fog."

By now, after Molly Gertrude had mulled over all the details, she was almost certain she knew what had transpired, but up till this point it was still only a theory. Nothing more.

Talking to Charmayne would hopefully help her to find that one puzzle piece that was still missing.

And it did.

Molly Gertrude had a very specific question for Abe's daughter, and when the girl gave her the answer Molly Gertrude was hoping for, she let out a deep sigh and leaned back on her chair, barely able to suppress a victorious smile.

"I think I know what happened to your Daddy, Charmayne," she said.

"What?" Charmayne leaned over the table and grabbed Molly Gertrude's hands.

"You must trust me, Charmayne," Molly Gertrude said. "It's too early to tell, but I will expose the people who are responsible for your father's misfortune on Saturday, during JJ Barnes' birthday party."

"You mean… there's more than one?"

Molly Gertrude did not answer her. Instead, she said, "Wait till the party, Charmayne. I have to be careful, and not all details are in place."

Disappointment flashed over Charmayne's face. "But I am not invited to Barnes' party."

"You are not?" Molly Gertrude took the list of invitees and

scanned it with her eyes. Then she nodded. "You are right. I don't see your name on the list. We'll have to change that." Molly Gertrude opened her drawer, pulled out a printed invitation and handed it to Charmayne. "Now, you are officially invited," she grinned.

Charmayne's eyes widened. "Can you invite whoever you want?"

"Yes, I can," Molly Gertrude chuckled. "JJ has put me in charge of inviting his guests." She smacked her lips. "There are a few others that are not on JJ Barnes' list, but they are people that I personally would really like to see at that party, too. Your Billy is one of them, and so is Albert Finney, and a few others..."

Charmayne looked puzzled. "Others? Like who?"

"There's an old friend of your father's. I would be honored if he would come too."

"Who is that?" Charmayne asked.

"Do you remember a man by the name of Willy Wilmot? I believe he's a dentist from Trenton Valley."

Surprise was etched on Charmayne's face. "Of course, I remember him." Her face darkened. "He was actually my Daddy's business partner during the time when Daddy was not walking the straight and narrow. When Daddy found faith in God, he left town almost instantly. He's an unpleasant fellow if you ask me." Charmayne wrinkled her nose. "Are you sure you want to invite him to Barnes' party? I am not looking forward to meeting him again."

"He goes by the name of Salvatore Swaggart now," Molly Gertrude explained, "but, trust me, it's good if he comes. I'll get him an invitation as well..."

"What if he doesn't want to come?"

"He'll come," Molly Gertrude gave Charmayne a mysterious smile. She cleared her throat and said, "Thank you for coming in, Charmayne. You have been a great help. Now if you will excuse me, I have to make a few more arrangements for Barnes' party. I still need to find a trustworthy waiter, and there are a few other details to take care of as well."

Charmayne nodded and pushed her chair away so she could get up. "You are speaking in mysteries, Miss Grey," she said as she rubbed her forehead, "but I will do as you ask, and trust you."

Molly Gertrude placed her hand on Charmayne's arm. "You asked me to find out what happened to your Daddy... And now I think I know." She narrowed her eyes as she peered into Charmayne's eyes. "But, we must play the game in just the right way, otherwise the bad guys may get nervous and then they may run, and we may never see them again."

Charmayne stared with big, round eyes at Molly Gertrude while she clutched her invitation to JJ Barnes' birthday party to her chest.

"Thank you, Miss Grey. I'll see you on Saturday night."

JJ Barnes was tickled pink as he scanned the living room from his elevated position on the little stage, right next to the Swaying Cornstalks, the local country band that Dora Brightside had been able to hire for the occasion. The jigging mass of people before him seemed to be enjoying themselves immensely. This party was much better than he had expected in his wildest dreams, and he needed to make sure to pay Molly Gertrude Grey and her Cozy Bridal Agency a hefty, extra bonus.

"I invited quite a few extra guests," Miss Grey had told him, "just so that we make this a most memorable birthday party for you and your wife." And she was right. Judging by the smiles on everyone's faces and the amount of booming laughter that could be heard from virtually every corner, JJ Barnes' party would go in the books as one of the top events in Calmhaven for this year. And the people of this town needed it, after the ruined wedding party and the unfortunate problems of Abe Mortimer their beloved mayor. People still did not know if Abe would pull through. Most thought he was pretty much dead and gone. For the few who were close enough to know anything about Abe's progress, there had been a few tentative signs the day before, but for the most part everyone's nerves were on edge and it was a relief to bring in a bit of laughter and relaxation.

"Enjoying the party, Sheriff?" A cheerful voice, barely audible above the riffs of the country guitars, caught his attention. Barnes turned and stared at the smiling face of the old woman who was responsible for organizing the party and who was heavily leaning on her walking cane.

"I am, Miss Grey. You and your assistant did a marvelous job." He cast her a warm smile. "I am sorry I have been a bit gruff with you, but really... you are much, much better at organizing parties than you are at real police work."

"I know," Molly Gertrude answered meekly. "Actually..." she raised her voice as the Swaying Cornstalks just began their country rendition of 'Can't Buy Me Love.' "...that's what I wanted to talk to you about." The noise became deafening.

"Oh, how is that?" Barnes called back.

"I still would like to give you a birthday present."

A warm smile appeared on JJ Barnes' face. "No need for that, Miss Grey. What can you give the man who already has everything?"

"How about a criminal?" Molly Gertrude tilted her head, hoping she would have sufficiently roused the Sheriff's attention.

His face darkened. "What do you mean, Miss Grey? This is my birthday." Barnes' good mood disappeared as fast as snow in the tropics. "Tonight, I don't want to be bothered with your conspiracy theories."

"But tonight is the night that I will expose the man who attempted to kill Abe Mortimer," Molly Gertrude fired back. "But I need your help."

The Sheriff wrinkled his nose. He didn't say anything.

"I think I can prove Abe Mortimer was ruthlessly targeted, Sheriff," Molly Gertrude went on. "Will you give me a chance?"

Barnes stared at Molly Gertrude for what seemed to be the longest time. At last he narrowed his eyes and hissed, "One chance, Miss Grey. Only one."

"Good," Molly Gertrude said. She seemed relieved. "Is there a quiet room where we can talk?"

"How about my study," Barnes replied. "Just the two of us?"

Molly Gertrude shook her head. "No. If you will ask Deputy Digby to round up the following persons, and bring them to your study." As she said it, she opened her handbag and pulled out a paper that contained several names and handed it to Sheriff Barnes.

"What's this?" Barnes asked as he took the list from Molly Gertrude.

"These are the people I would like to see together," Molly Gertrude explained.

The Sheriff read the list.

"Salvatore Swaggart?" He looked up. "Who is he, and what is he doing at my party?"

"He'll tell you himself," Molly Gertrude answered. "And do you see that waiter over there?" She pointed to a tall man who was standing stiffly near the table with snacks and drinks in a starched white shirt and a black bow tie.

Barnes peered at the man. "What about him? That fellow is in need of a haircut," he smirked as he noticed the man's rather wild hair. It covered most of his forehead, and his bushy eyebrows were wild. What made him even stranger were his tiny spectacles, with the rather dark glasses, that covered his eyes.

Barnes turned back to Molly Gertrude. "Couldn't you have hired a waiter that was a bit more sophisticated? Next time, don't go for the cheapest deals, Miss Grey."

"There's a reason he is here, Sheriff," Molly Gertrude said. "Just get him into your study as well."

Barnes narrowed his eyes. "All right, Miss Grey. Just this once, but if you don't have something really amazing to show me... you may be sorry you organized this party."

"I will not let you down, Sheriff," Molly Gertrude said. "Just trust me."

18

SOLVING THE CASE

"**W**hat am I doing here?" Billy Monroe asked Deputy Digby as the police man directed him to a seat in the corner of Barnes' study.

Digby shrugged his shoulders. "Don't rightfully know, Billy. I am just doing what my boss told me." He turned around again and stepped past the waiter with the messy hair, who stood in the corner next to a tray of drinks, and disappeared back into the hallway.

"Yeah, it's the JJ Barnes special," Alfred Finney piped up with a scowl from a seat opposite of Billy's. "I thought the party was pretty good, until they ushered me in here too. What's going on?"

"Let's all be calm," Charmayne suggested. "Miss Molly Gertrude Grey told me she wanted to talk to us. She said she wanted to solve the mystery of Abe Mortimer's misfortune."

"Miss Molly Gertrude Grey again?" Finney said with clear disdain. "We all know Abe's brush with death was an accident." He turned his face to Dora, who stood in her flowing evening dress right next to the open fire place, and demanded an answer. "You are working with Molly Gertrude. What's going on?"

Dora shook her head. "She hasn't told me, Mister Finney. I suggest, we just wait and see."

The door opened again and Digby returned, this time with Salvatore Swaggert and pointed to an empty seat near the window. "Please, sit over there."

Both Finney and Charmayne looked surprised at seeing the man, but Swaggart resisted their stares, leaned back in his seat and pulled out a cigar. After he lit it, he blew out carefully formed circles of smoke and glared at the others. "Why are we here?"

Finney frowned. "I had not expected to see you here, Salvatore."

Upon hearing the name Salvatore, Charmayne arched her brows, but decided not to say anything.

"I got this urgent mail, I was needed here," Swaggart hissed, but I am now led to believe it's all been a big hoax and that somebody is fooling us."

Once more the door opened. This time JJ Barnes himself entered, followed by Molly Gertrude Grey.

Upon seeing Molly Gertrude, Finney blurted out in an angry voice, "What's going on? I thought this was a party. It looks more like an interrogation."

"Quiet," Barnes barked. "Miss Molly Gertrude here claims she knows what happened to Abe Mortimer."

"We all know what happened to him." Finney was in an obstinate mood. "This mess is not very good for my business. I don't for a moment believe he choked on my cake anyways. It's a slur on my good name. The old goat had a heart attack I bet. I think my reputation has suffered enough, and I don't want to have to be subjected to more nonsense from this old lady. I suggest you move her to a nursing home as soon as possible." He got up with the intent of leaving the study, but Digby stepped in, and placed his firm hand on Finney's shoulder. "Sit down, Albert. You are not excused."

Molly Gertrude Grey cleared her throat. "I am really sorry to have you all gathered here, but I am absolutely convinced Abe Mortimer's unfortunate encounter with supposedly deadly cake was not an accident, but that some unscrupulous character tried to kill him. What's more, I believe those responsible is right here among us."

That information caused a stir in the room. All eyes were now on Molly Gertrude.

"There are four of us here, not including you, Sheriff

Barnes and Deputy Digby," Charmayne cried out. She looked around, a little white in the face.

"That's right," Molly Gertrude added. "There's you and Billy, there's Albert Finney... and there's our good dentist Salvatore Swaggart..." She let her voice trail off, "... or shall I call you Willy Wilmot? After all, that is how Charmayne knows you."

Swaggart scowled. "You've got nothing on me, lady. There's no law against changing your name. I needed a fresh start after all the lies in Calmhaven. I figured a new name would help."

"Of course," Molly Gertrude said with a small nod. "I understand. And that's not why you are here."

"So, why *am* I here?" Swaggart blew out another blue cloud of smoke. "I've got nothing to do with Abe Mortimer. In fact, I wasn't even present at that wretched wedding." His eyes flashed with dark hatred.

For a moment it was absolutely still in the room. Nobody dared to say a word.

"Let me explain," Molly Gertrude said at last, and she turned to Billy.

"My first suspect was Billy."

All eyes turned to Billy who shifted uneasily on his chair. "I loved Abe," Billy squealed. "I had nothing to do with this."

"But you are heavily in debt, aren't you Billy?" Molly

Gertrude stated, as she stared at Billy. "And you were hoping Abe Mortimer's wealth would help you to clear them…"

"I did," Billy confessed while his eye began to twitch, "But, I was going to ask Abe for a loan. That's all. I loved Abe."

Molly Gertrude nodded. "It's common knowledge that both, you and Abe, were not always such model citizens. Of course Abe changed when he joined Papa Julian's church, and he became like a father to you… although you, Billy, still kept on gambling and you collected enormous debts."

Tears sprang out of Billy's eyes. "I am sorry, but I really had nothing to do with Abe's…" Billy's voice tailed off to silence.

"Maybe not," Molly Gertrude said, but from the way she said it, it was clear Molly Gertrude was displeased with Billy. "I also investigated Albert Finney," she went on.

"What a waste of time," Finney fired back. "I had nothing to do with it. Why in the world would I jeopardize my business? My cake was clean. There was not a trace of poison in it. "

"There are more ways to murder a man than by putting poison in a cake," Molly Gertrude fired back.

"But, I am not even in the will. I have no motive."

"Actually, you do," Molly Gertrude replied in a firm voice. "You are still in love with Charmayne, and you hated the fact that Abe allowed his daughter to marry Billy, the man you despise from the depth of your heart. And was not that first mouthful intended for the groom?"

"Lies. This is outrageous," Finney cried out. "I want a lawyer."

Molly Gertrude didn't listen, and simply went on with her observations. "Actually, my suspicion rose when I happened to bump into you at the dental office in Trenton Valley, the clinic of Swaggart, and he handed you an envelope full of aspirin… "

Bewilderment flashed over Finney's face. "You were there… in Trenton Valley?"

"We were Albert," Molly Gertrude replied. "And as you may know, the doctor's did find traces of aspirin in Abe Mortimer's saliva."

A cry erupted from Charmayne's throat. Before anyone knew what was happening, she jumped up, ran over to Albert Finney and began to pummel the startled man with both of her fists. "You horrible, wicked man… *You* did it. *You* tried to kill my Daddy. You were jealous, and mad at my father for allowing Billy to marry me, instead of you."

Digby rushed forward and pulled Charmayne away from Finney. The man stared with round, wide eyes at Charmayne and then slouched over in his chair. "I didn't try to kill, Abe," he mumbled. "It's all a mistake. I want a lawyer."

Charmayne began to weep, and while Digby prevented

her from battering Finney, she pointed a trembling finger at the cake maker. "You knew my Daddy was allergic to aspirin. I told you that myself. Very few people knew about that. Even the slightest bit of aspirin would cause him to go into anaphylaxis. You killed him." She howled hysterically again.

"I did not feed Abe any aspirin... I needed it for myself."

"I know," Molly Gertrude agreed. "I did some checking on your dental records. And you are having all your teeth pulled."

Albert Finney blushed.

"You've been eating too much of your own sugary concoctions, and you are now paying the price. The aspirin you've been given by Swaggart was only to help you to combat the pain after all your teeth were pulled out."

"I-eh..." Finney stammered. "It's true. I went to Swaggart in Trenton Valley, as I didn't think having rotting teeth was a very good advertisement for my cake making business."

"And that...," Molly Gertrude said as she turned to Salvatore Swaggart who was still forming perfect circles with the smoke he blew out, "...leaves you, Mr. Swaggart."

The dentist stared with a defiant look at Molly Gertrude. If he could have had the power to crush Molly Gertrude as if she were nothing but an annoying ant, he would have instantly done it.

"You were buddies in crime, Swaggart," Molly Gertrude said with a scowl. "You and Abe used young kids for your dirty plans, supposedly as an organization that was helping orphans, foundlings and castaways. You even got an award from the Calmhaven city-department for your so-called good works…"

Swaggart's eyes flashed, but he said nothing.

"Here's the proof," Molly Gertrude said, and she pulled out the photograph that Billy had given her. She handed the picture to JJ Barnes who stared at it with fascination. "This is a picture of you getting an award, but it was all lies. You never did a thing for these poor children, but you and Abe only used them. But then Abe changed…"

Molly Gertrude motioned for the waiter to give her some water. The man walked over and respectfully handed her a glass.

After Molly Gertrude took a few sips she continued. "Abe Mortimer was sick and tired of being a crook. He confessed everything when he joined Papa Julian's church, and even served a year for some of his crimes. He was genuinely sorry. He stopped his criminal life, of which Billy was a part, and he turned good. From that day forward he only lived to undo the evil the two of you had committed. He also tried to convince his former buddies to stop their wicked lives as well, which is why he took such an interest in Billy."

"It's a nice little bedtime story," Swaggart scoffed. "And then there came a big, fat gray elephant with a big snout who blew magical fairy dust over the land and all the children fell into a happy sleep." He shook his head in disgust and let out a curse.

The others stared at him, shocked at his language.

"There's no elephant, Swaggart," Molly Gertrude hissed. "Abe Mortimer gave you a chance to repent, but you did not care. You never changed. Abe Mortimer was tired of your unrepentant life style and he was going to the police."

Swaggart, feeling awfully sure of himself, chuckled. "Where's the proof, old woman? You've got nothing on me."

"We got this," Molly Gertrude said. She opened her purse again and pulled out Abe Mortimer's diary that Charmayne had given to her.

"What's that?" Swaggart asked, while he narrowed his eyes.

"It's a diary. Abe Mortimer's diary... He mentions you several times."

"The bungling words of an old man," Swaggart jeered. "That's no proof,"

"Shall I read you some passages?" Molly Gertrude suggested in a meek voice. "There are some passages here in which he claims he was going to talk to the police, giving them names, dates and places about the crimes the two of you committed. He didn't really want to rat on you, he just wanted you to stop using innocent young people. Simply put, he wanted you to stop being a crook. And the..." she leafed through the diary, "... he gave you an ultimatum. Two weeks before someone tried to kill him, but you did not heed it."

She pulled another piece of paper out of her bag. "Ever see this?" She unfolded it for all to see. It was the threat that Charmayne had found in her Daddy's drawer.

Stay out of my life, or else...

"I've never seen that weird paper in my life," Swaggart shrugged his shoulders.

"Come on, man," JJ Barnes's angry voice boomed through the room. "I never thought much of Miss Molly Gertrude's accusations, but this is getting interesting."

"Oh is it?" Swaggart fought back. "I wasn't even present at the wedding. You are all narrow-minded idiots. This is nothing but a witch hunt to discredit my legal dental work."

"Is it?" Molly Gertrude fired back. "Then let me tell you how you set out to kill Abe," Molly Gertrude said.

"You knew Abe Mortimer couldn't stand aspirin. He had told you so himself. But there was more than that. He had an intolerance for nuts as well. Nothing serious. Just a mild reaction, but whenever Abe Mortimer would eat nuts he would start to cough."

"So?" Swaggart said with a scowl.

"When he ate the cake, there were nuts in it. Of course, as a result, Abe coughed. Not because he choked on the cake, but because of the ground-up nuts in the cake. Thankfully, there was a very kind waiter, who ran up to help poor Abe. This kind waiter offered him some wine to flush away the so-called cake in his air passage."

"Nice story," Swaggart shook his head.

"Except," Molly Gertrude went on, "this waiter was not as kind as he pretended to be. He had put aspirin in the wine before he gave it to Abe. As soon as Abe drank it, his heart stopped working as it should. I checked this with the doctor. Aspirin is harmless, except for those people who have a condition as Abe Mortimer had."

For a long moment, nobody said a word.

"He should have died instantly," Molly Gertrude said at last with a sigh, "but old Abe is not one to give up without a fight!"

"Well, *I* wasn't there," Swaggart said, as he got up. "I have an alibi for that day. I was with my patients in Trenton Valley."

"Sit down," Digby hissed. "We will tell you when to leave."

Swaggart shook his head in disgust, but lowered himself

back into his seat. "Another policeman on a power trip," he mumbled as he cast Digby an angry glare.

"Of course, you weren't there," Molly Gertrude went on. "You never get your hands dirty. You let other people take care of your dirty work."

"You do not know what you are talking about," Swaggart hissed. "You are speaking nonsense."

Molly Gertrude motioned with her hand for the waiter to give her some more water. The man stepped over with his tray. But, just as he went to hand Molly Gertrude another glass, Molly Gertrude, with a fast movement of her hand, pulled on the waiter's hair.

"W-What are you doing, Miss Grey," Charmayne gasped. The waiter let out a yelp as he dropped the glass of water and stared in bewilderment at Molly Gertrude.

He was bald.

Instantly, he jerked the wig back out of Molly Gertrude's hands, but everyone had seen what had happened. The man stared for a panic-stricken moment at Molly Gertrude, and then ran for the door.

"Grab him Digby," Molly Gertrude shouted.

Instantly Digby sprang into action, as if he were a professional football player, and threw himself on top of the waiter, tackled him and held him down in an iron grip.

"Meet George Latimer," Molly Gertrude said as she knelt

down next to Digby and the waiter and pulled the man's glasses off his nose as well, and removed his fake eyebrows. "Here is Billy's old buddy in crime, and Swaggart's present errand boy. We thought these hairy caterpillars were false moustaches," Molly waved the limp fake eyebrows in her fingers, "but they are eyebrows designed to compliment your many alter-egos."

"George?" Billy jumped up, as he recognized his former friend. "I can't believe this, Is this true? Did you really try to kill Abe?"

"I am sorry, Billy," George cried out. "You know how it is… I just couldn't get out of it."

JJ Barnes let out a soft cry. "What horrors! And that in Calmhaven."

Molly Gertrude spoke to Bald-Head, who stared at her from the floor with fearful eyes. "From the moment I first saw you in Miss Marmelotte's Tearoom," she said, "I knew I had seen you before. I just didn't know where, but then it came to me. You were also the waiter at the wedding party. Swaggart had gotten you into the wedding and knew about the nuts. He told you to be ready. As soon as Abe would start coughing, you were supposed to give him the aspirin infested wine. A smart move it was. No real poison. It was almost the perfect murder… but the brain behind it wasn't you, George… That was Salvatore Swaggart, alias Willy Wilmot. You were even able to sweep away the evidence pretending to clean up the broken glass. Very clever indeed!"

But, in all the commotion nobody had been watching Swaggart. The man had pulled a gun out of his coat pocket.

"Everybody back," he shouted in a hoarse voice. "Up against the wall, hands behind your heads."

"Don't," JJ Barnes hissed. "The show is over, Swaggart. The whole state is going to be on the lookout for you."

"I'll take my chances," Swaggart fumed. "Come on... Hurry. Up against the wall."

Billy, Finney and Charmayne got up from their seats and slowly moved their noses towards the wall. "You too, Digby," he spat out the words.

Digby released his grip on Bald-Head and got up on his legs.

"It's all right," Barnes mumbled from the side. "Do as he says."

"That's right," Swaggart huffed. "You too, Molly Gertrude Grey and Officer Barnes."

At that instant the door was thrown open wide, and Miss Tilly appeared in the door. She was holding a glass of champagne, and stared with hazy eyes at the scene before her. "I-eh- So-Sorry," she slurred. "Looking for the ba-ba-bathroom."

But George Latimer saw his chance.

He knew the gig was up, and he no longer wanted to

dance to the tunes of Willy Wilmot, or Salvatore Swaggart.

In one swift move he forced himself up to his knees and while Miss Tilly ran off screaming, he jumped on Swaggart like a tiger. Both men fell backwards and crashed to the floor. Digby knew he should not wait for even a second, and he too jumped forwards.

A shot sounded.

Bald-Head screamed in pain and stared in horror at his leg. "I am hit..." he screamed. "Help me!" The gun had gone off and Swaggart had shot him in the leg. But it was Swaggart's last deed as Digby was way too strong for the dentist and forced the gun out of his hand.

"Call an ambulance," Digby yelled. Then he turned back to Swaggart and hissed in his ear, "I think we've got more than enough evidence on you to put you away for more than twenty years."

"Good work, Digby," Barnes mumbled to Digby. Then he turned to the others and said, "Go join the party... It's over. I got it all under control and will take it from here."

Molly Gertrude sank down on a chair. She was as white as a sheet.

"Are you all right?" Dora asked.

"I think so, dear," she nodded as she looked up at Dora and cast her a weak smile. "That is quite enough excitement for one day."

"Thanks for the birthday present," JJ Barnes told Molly Gertrude as he stepped out the door, hauling Swaggart along. "I am glad I was able to solve this troublesome case. Calmhaven can sleep safely again."

Molly just nodded. No words came. At last, she turned to Dora and asked, "Do you mind driving me home, Dora. I would like to see Misty."

"No problem, Miss Molly. Let's go. I could use a cup of your raspberry tea, and I wouldn't mind having a Silky Citrus Curd Cookie."

Molly Gertrude smiled. "You can have 10 of them, Dora. You deserve every one of them."

19

ALL'S WELL THAT ENDS WELL

"**W**ould you mind being the Godmother of our baby, Miss Molly Gertrude?"

Molly Gertrude frowned as she stared at Charmayne. "But I am in my seventies, Charmayne. How can I be a good Godmother?"

Charmayne pressed her lips together. "The Bridal Agency then. You and Dora can both be godmothers. Will you please do me and Billy the honor?"

Molly Gertrude threw up her hands and smiled. "How can I refuse, Charmayne. When is the baby due?"

Charmayne rubbed her tummy. "The doctor says it will be another two months."

"I am so glad for the two of you," Molly Gertrude whispered. "And you are feeling fine?"

"Couldn't be any better," Charmayne replied. "Billy is doing well. He found a job at Tykes Lumberyard. He's almost done paying off his debts, and since we have joined Papa Julian's Bible studies for married couples, our married life is getting better every day."

"I am so happy to hear that," Molly Gertrude said as she squeezed Charmayne's hand. "And how about my dear friend? How is he doing after such a scare?"

Charmayne looked at Molly Gertrude with a warm expression. "Daddy is doing fine, Miss Molly. He came round the very day you exposed his would-be killers. It took a few weeks for him to regain his strength, but since then he's been stronger and more intent on changing the world for good than ever before. It's a bone-fide miracle, Miss Molly."

"Well, my dear girl, we most certainly believe in those. The good Lord is a miracle worker in all of our lives!"

"Things really couldn't be any better than they are at the moment. Thank you for helping me Miss Molly Gertrude. When I saw Daddy keel over that day, I just knew something was wrong, and I could only think of one person to go to. And that person was you, Miss Molly Gertrude Grey." Charmayne smiled.

Molly Gertrude shrugged. "I am just running a Bridal Agency. That's all."

Charmayne chuckled. "You should change the name to the Snoopy Bridal Agency, or something like that. You and

Dora make a great team, and Calmhaven can't do it without the two of you."

Molly Gertrude smiled. "Hey… you want one of my Chocolate Delights. My new batch is just about ready, and you can be the judge of whether or not I put too much sugar in them. Want to try?"

"I'd love to Miss Molly Gertrude. Probably good for my baby too."

Molly Gertrude got up from her seat and disappeared into the kitchen. Charmayne inhaled the luscious scent of the chocolate cookies and smiled. "Thank you, God, for your goodness. Thank you for Billy, and Daddy, and for dear Molly and Dora."

Dora, who had been quietly sitting listening added one more note of gratitude to Charmayne's heartfelt prayer.

"And thank you, Lord, for chocolate delights!"

In unison, Charmayne and Dora giggled their "amen" as Molly stepped back through the door with a tray filled with chocolate covered manna from heaven.

Love Molly's adventures? Why not join our PureRead Mystery Readers Club and receive free cozy mystery books, New Releases and other special offers? It's completely free! To sign up just go to PureRead.com/cozy-mystery-club

ABOUT PUREREAD

T hank you for reading!

Here at PureRead we aim to serve you, our dear reader, with good, clean Christian stories. You can be assured that any PureRead book you pick up will not only be hugely enjoyable, but free of any objectionable content.

We are deeply thankful to you for choosing our books. Your support means that we can continue to provide stories just like the one you have just read.

PLEASE LEAVE A REVIEW

Please do consider leaving a review for this book on Amazon - something as simple as that can help others just like you discover and enjoy the books we publish, and your reviews are a constant encouragement to our hard working writers.

OUR EXCLUSIVE READERCLUB (FREE TO JOIN)

If you would like to hear about new titles, free books and special offers by our team of talented PureRead authors be sure to sign up and **become part of our Exclusive Reader Club. It's quick, easy and 100% free.**

SIGN UP NOW at PureRead.com/cozy-mystery-club

LIKE OUR PUREREAD COZY MYSTERY FACEBOOK PAGE

Love Facebook? We do too and PureRead has a very special Facebook page where we keep in touch with readers.

To like and follow PureRead on Facebook go to **www.facebook.com/purereadmystery**

OUR WEBSITE

To browse all of our PureRead books visit our website at PureRead.com

Made in the USA
Lexington, KY
07 July 2019